Kind words about *ETERNITY: The ~~Long and~~ Short of It*

"William Brandon's *Eternity: The ~~Long and~~ Short of It* is a wonderfully smart and merciless dystopian collection about the evils of our times. With Ballardian scalpel-precision in dialogues and situations, William Brandon dissects the rotten limbs of neoliberalism, bigotry and technology in order to present us with the monster we have created ourselves. Terrifically well written and constructed, *Eternity* is a must-read for all those who seek a rewarding challenge in a book. Totally recommended."

— Seb Doubinsky, author of *Missing Signal*, *The Invisible* and *Paperclip*

"An intriguing blend of sci-fi and horror, these stories smash together the future we were promised and the very different future we live with now. The world of *Eternity* is dystopian and paranoid, but not without a thread of soul that pulls you through."

— Scott Gilbertson, luxagraf.net

"Brandon's ability to merge a great story with near-future SF and technology is impressive enough, but when combined with real-world-politicking *Eternity* becomes far more than just a collection of great, interconnected stories; it's a clear warning about the endless ways corporations seek to own us, and the ways in which a daily grind can make us numb to the

bigger picture. Fans of *Black Mirror* should run—not walk—to buy this book."

— Lindz McLeod, author of *Turducken* and *Beast*

"William M. Brandon III's *Eternity* deftly depicts a world gone whorled, where isolatos and desperados, worker bees and wannabes career through odd careers like post-Rapture-messaging-service server farmer, call-center-for-monetized-conversations operator, desire-for-new-products test driver, etc., each wildly imaginative story both mirror to our terrible present and medium to terrifying futures—from here to eternity, in other words. Keenly attacking disaster capitalism, total-spectrum surveillance, apocalyptic cults, religious fundamentalism, and more, *Eternity* foregrounds the following ironies: the more connection, the less intimacy; the more light, the less illumination; the more information, the less understanding."

— John Madera, author of *Nervosities* and *Among the Dynamos*

"A young atheist navigating the rise of American Christofascism and a secret police of Christian hardliners. A refugee adrift in a cyberpunk landscape looking for salvation. An apocalypse cult underpinning the American political-industrial complex, awaiting its Lovecraftian god. Poverty, avarice, desperation. Brandon's interconnected tales—character-driven but dripping with commentary—are missives from post-Trump America, a bullhorn raised at our nihilism and apathy, warning that decline isn't coming: 'It's been here for a long time.'"

— Brandon Getz, author of *Stop Me If You've Heard This One Before*

"*Eternity* is a collection of warnings from William M. Brandon III. This punk philosopher has been transmitting warnings through his novels for the better part of the last decade, and those who have heard have heeded. With this collection of stories (or are they essays, or does it matter? Why do you even ask? Are you a cop?), he breaks his vision down even further with easier chunks for chewing, while still dense in righteous nutrition. Genre is just another authority for Brandon to defy with relish, and that deliciousness is shared with the reader. In *Eternity*, William Brandon cuts through the corruption and hypocrisy inherent in the American Experience with a skeptic's scalpel. This is not a reading experience; this is a rallying cry!"

— Jordan A. Rothacker, author of *The Pit, and No Other Stories*, and the forthcoming novel, *The Shrieking of Nothing*

"William Brandon shapes Athens, Georgia as Kafka shaped Prague. The fabric of reality is, indeed, thin and the ever-present threat of detection by an underground THEM is as close to the characters of these stories as though THEY were standing just behind them, breathing thinly and waiting for the right moment to strike.

Eternity features hellish call centers and data uploading facilities, the individuals who pick up jobs at these places to avoid a hideous fate, and the toxic blend of faith and misinformation. In William Brandon's Georgia, beware. You are being watched."

— Pam Jones, author of *A Carnival of Birds*, *The Arizona Room*, and *Andermatt County: Two Parables*

"William Brandon's newest collection *Eternity: The ~~Long and~~ Short of It*, is written with a blistering, brilliant urgency, whose primary function, outlined as a compelling series of 'warnings,' offers readers a remarkably thoughtful insight into class disparity, privatization, the colossal totality of civilization as information control, land ownership, disaster capitalism, history, the absurd reflective technological investigations of a rapturous theology of the doomed, marginalization, as well as the monopolization/control/management of the earth, including the reality in which it orbits, where we are all condemned as consumable objects, measured simply as an enterprise of assets to be managed by the elite.

"Brandon's fiction dares to help readers, grappling with the existential perils associated with navigating the contemporary tribulations perpetually imbedded within 'capital R, Reality,' to not only help us understand the places that we have been, but more importantly, examine the possible positions of the paths that our civilization may take us, if we fail to collectively course correct, as we strive to more positively model the sharper coming curves of our ongoing evolution.

"It is rare that a work of fiction can not only serve as deeply insightful, compassionate, caring, and forward thinking, but it also serves as a clarion call of solidarity that invites readers to unify around the idea that we use our arts as a means to create real measurable paradigmatic social change, it is for this reason that Brandon is not just an author, but also a creative pioneer, working for the themes of resistance and revolution, for as the book comes to a close we quickly realize that it is everything that we love that is on the line that we must collectively, not only fight for, but live to forever protect and preserve."

— Phillip Freedenberg, author of *America and the Cult of the Cactus Boots: A Diagnostic*

"What Brandon has done here, in such Brandon fashion, is weave together the daily terror of American Existence into an oppressive, but elevated tapestry. We have the terror of work, and the way offices are torture chambers-slash-competitive leagues-slash-eugenics laboratories. We have the combined legacy of old culture and banality of individual tragedy. We have religion and its confidence games blending with technology and its own confidence games. The warnings are haunting and the way Brandon blends sci-fi, horror, technophilia/phobia and dystopian cyberpunk themes creates something beautiful."

— Nate Ragolia, author of *One Person Can't Make a Difference* and *There You Feel Free*

books and stories by
William M. Brandon III

SILENCE and Selene
The Exile The Matriarch & The Flood
Welcome to Spring Street
"The Atlantic"

ETERNITY

The ~~Long and~~ Short of It

the collected warnings of
William M. Brandon III

Denver, Colorado

Published in the United States by:
Spaceboy Books LLC
1627 Vine Street
Denver, CO 80206
www.readspaceboy.com

Cover image: M87 supermassive black hole
Image credit: Event Horizon Telescope Collaboration

'The Atheist and The Rapture Button' first appeared in "BONED Every Which Way 2019" (Spaceboy Books, 2019)

ISBN: 978-1-951393-27-4
First printed December 2023

for
god's victims

With very special thanks to...
C. Lee, QL, and The Captain of all Captains.
HE IS BIRTHDAY!

herein

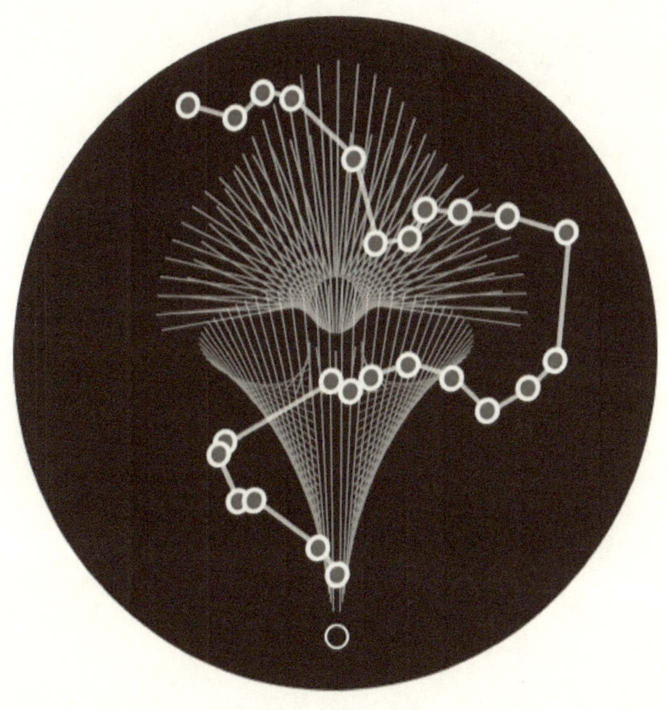

For me, it is far better to grasp the Universe as it really is than to persist in delusion, however satisfying and reassuring.

— Carl Sagan

A Unifying Field

Everyone is a database entry
waiting to be observed.

The drive for total information awareness is an attempt by the universe to understand itself; it is the seminal glance at what omniscience would look/be like. We are damned to ignorance, trapped trying to filter the constant information, because:

- we are not the "whole," we are cells/nodes
- "consciousness" is the nervous system of the universe, blindly collecting and analyzing data
- by deign of self-awareness, we strive to learn and react to the mute apathy of stars

But The Earth—
a deep flaw;
a secluded and isolated bundle of nerves—
is incapable of communicating

with the rest of the body.

The Atheist &
The Rapture Button

thegreenestpasture.org

I

Work is morally compromising. For some, that compromise means retail slavery during the holidays, or slinging drinks for ungrateful inebriated scum. For others, it means protecting something so deeply wrong that we can never be forgiven. My name is Declan by the way, and it's probably a good sign that you are still able to read this.

I'd been searching for more freelance work, but the listings offered only warehouse jobs, wait staff positions, and catering shifts. Though I was desperate enough to take any job I could find, none came within miles of paying my rent. I'd have to take two (sometimes three) of the offered positions to break even. Then, everything changed:

> *Seeking a Systems Administrator in Hollywood, Ca. Full-time position overseeing complex multi-state customer database and product quality assurance. Must be willing to be on call 24/7. Contact Greg Bahnsen at (469) 282-4464.*

I knew my way around a server, but I had no formal training. I felt confident I could tap-dance my way through the interview, start high on salary, and let them back me down. I had to try, it was a quick path to solvency.

I dialed the number in the ad.

"You have reached Greg Bahnsen. Please leave your name, number, and a short message after the tone. Thank you and God bless."

tone

"Hello, Mr. Bahnsen. My name is Declan Holyoake and I am calling in regard to your advertised position for a Systems Administrator. I have nearly a decade's worth of experience maintaining databases for large and small organizations. I can be reached at (213) 382-5968. I look forward to hearing from you."

I nailed the voicemail.

Jenny, my landlord, called up from her meager backyard.

"Hey, you got a second?"

I descended the spiral staircase from my attic apartment to a narrow strip of landscaped rock and concrete behind Jenny's Hollywood bungalow.

"Hey, are you still looking for work?"

A difficult conversation to have with your landlord. My phone vibrated: *Mom.* I pointed the screen at Jenny and she waved me off, Mom could wait.

"I'm always looking for more work."

"We need a doorman on Monday nights at the bar, there's probably two shifts per week that you could pick up."

My phone stopped vibrating. "I have an interview this week that seems really promising." That was a lie. "But I'll stop by regardless." Two lies.

"It's all good; I was just curious." Her lie was the hat trick.

I lit a cigarette to avoid eye contact as Jenny started to walk back into the house. "By the way, have you seen that fucking cat around?"

I kept lying, "Not lately." Jenny had murder on her mind.

"I poured a ton of bleach in the flower bed; if he shits in there again it'll be the last time."

I stared at Jenny with all due horror as I dialed Mom. "Hey, sorry 'bout that. How are you feeling today?"

"I am ok. Every day is a little better." Mom's voice had taken on a plodding, childlike quality after her stroke.

"Your speech is improving."

"Thank you. I try." Mom laughed. "When are you coming to visit?"

The answer was complicated. Rent was on the horizon and I was nowhere near covering it. "As soon as possible, Momma."

"I miss you. All I have for company is the internet and old tv shows."

"Rough life eh?"

She couldn't stop laughing. "Ok, I am feeling a little tired, so I will go. I love you."

"I love you too, Momma."

"God bless you."

I hung up.

⚔

Pathos was the only bar in Hollywood without a television, making it a sacred reprieve from the constant din of my viewpoint vs. your viewpoint. Some nut had ripped the bar's flatscreen from its mooring during the 2016 election, and the locals agreed that change was good. By the time Greg returned my call I'd been at Pathos a few hours and had four pints of stout in me. I hesitated. A non-answer could be a deal breaker, so even though I was getting bleary-eyed, I took the call.

"Good evening. Is this Mr. Bahnsen?"

"Why yes it is, um..."

"Declan."

"Yes, of course. Declan, please call me Greg. Thank you for answering my call. It is very important, as the ad mentioned, that I be able to reach you at critical times day and night."

"I understand."

As I walked out of Pathos, someone whispered over my shoulder: *Perfect. Good move, Declan.* It could have been anyone in the crowded dive.

I leaned against a wall outside. Hollywood Boulevard was busy for a Monday night in

January. Back then, Hollywood Boulevard was rarely quiet.

"Declan, I represent a large non-denominational church in Dallas, Texas..."

I was afraid of that...

"...and we are the proud sponsors of The Greenest Pasture program. Are you, by any chance, familiar with our work?"

"No sir, I'm not, but I am willing to learn."

"That's just fine. Let me ask you, what do you think of Jesus?"

"Honestly, I try not to if I can help it." It was either vocational suicide or a great ice breaker.

Greg laughed heartily. "Yes, yes, that's perfect, Declan. I feel like you are already a very strong contender for this position. Let's schedule a time for you to come into the office. Are you free this Thursday?"

—it was Tuesday. "Yes sir, I am; all day presently."

"Good, good. Let's say 10am, at 1680 Vine Street, Suite 1212. Does that work?"

"Yes sir, Thank you Mr. Bahn...I mean Greg. I really appreciate this opportunity."

"Don't thank me yet."

I sensed his smile on the other end of the line.

✄

I woke, shaved, and showered before 9am. A letter from Mom poked out of the small mailbox on my landlord's porch, so I snatched it for the walk. Between puffs of smoke, I read about Mom's high school classmates getting together for an informal reunion. She expressed surprise and delight that most of them had stayed god-fearing Americans.

Mom didn't have much in her life anymore beyond social media. I couldn't tell if loneliness was to blame for her revived spiritual fervor, or if she had reverted to her backward upbringing because it numbed the pain of paralysis. Mom had always been churchy, but she seemed to be falling in with the fever of the moment.

She mentioned making a big purchase: *with my not-married heathen son in mind. *sloppy smiley face* It set us back a little bit, but I want you to know how much I love you.* Her writing became less legible as the letter progressed. I folded it and placed it in my pocket.

An intense little man blocked the doorway of 1680 Vine Street. He wanted to know what my business was, and I thought I detected a military background in his pugnacious demeanor. Once I mentioned Greg and he reviewed his clipboard, the man relaxed and showed me to the elevator with a puppy dog's submissive geniality.

The Taft Building was beautiful. The lobby ceiling was vibrantly painted and trimmed, and the floors were greying marble. Decommissioned copper mail chutes lined the walls of the lobby. I examined one and was disappointed that it was bolted shut. I can imagine that people were tempted to put all manner of nonsense into those chutes in the age of email, but it was still a shame. The rickety elevator rolled slowly to the twelfth floor and I made a mental note to take the stairs when possible.

The door to suite 1212 lay at the south end of the long hallway and had chipped, recently re-applied, white paint covering it from frame to hinge to threshold. I knocked carefully but confidently on the door and a man answered.

"Come in, Declan, I'm Greg." Greg was one of those poor chaps who ages faster than nature intended. Though his baby face said late twenties, his jowls and receding hairline screamed just shy of sixty.

"I'll give you the grand tour. This will be your station," Greg pointed to a large desk equipped with a modern desktop PC and several file organizers. "Here is the server room," Greg pointed to a room buzzing with equipment and air conditioning systems. "And I'm in the back near the fire escape."

Greg's office was barren save for another large desk, a similar desktop PC, and no signs of actual work.

"I'm only here to make sure the Systems Admin. is comfortable and competent. Then, I make my way back to Texas." Greg gestured to a small round table in the corner of his office. "Please have a seat." He folded his hands over a stack of documents. "I only have a few routine questions for you. First, are you a member of any local worship centers or worship organizations?"

"No sir." I figured honesty was still the best policy, although pretending to be a bible-thumper did cross my mind.

"Excellent. Any church activities at all?"

"No sir."

"Out of laziness, or..." He let the question hang.

"I'm what you might call a practicing atheist, Greg."

Greg's eyes lit up. "Perfect! Do you have any problems with signing a non-disclosure agreement?"

"None whatsoever."

"Splendid. Let's get that out of the way before we proceed. I think you are our man, Declan." Greg smiled: just shy of a used car salesman and slightly more devious than your run-of-the-mill proselytizer.

"I need to ask one further question. Are you willing to be on-call twenty-four hours per day and seven days per week?"

"Yes."

"We require that you move into this facility. The office suite down the hall has been equipped with requisite sleeping and cooking arrangements; consider it a perk of the job. You will receive full health benefits, and a salary of one hundred thousand dollars before taxes."

My jaw dropped.

"You will be responsible for maintaining this office and all of its paperwork while I am away, but your primary responsibility will be to make sure they," Greg pointed to the server room, "keep running day and night. You will remain onsite from 8am until 5pm in case we have any unexpected visitors, or if I need your assistance in some way. The keypad for the server room requires a retinal scan. Any questions so far?"

"Yes, what are the servers running?"

"They maintain the database and operational data for The Greenest Pasture."

"The suspense is killing me," I joked.

"As a formality, I'd like to officially offer you the position before we discuss the program's details."

"Thank you, Greg! I accept wholeheartedly."

"Wonderful, then it's official, welcome to the family. I can be forthcoming now; part of the reason I chose you is that you are an atheist."

"I was getting that impression. Churches don't usually hire dirty heathens do they?"

"This job is a bit different. Years ago, our founder recognized that there were millions of believers who were born and raised in the church that would be left behind by the Rapture: husbands and wives, sons and daughters, Mayors and Presidents. Do you know what the Rapture is?"

"Yes, my Mom is a dyed-in-the-wool Southern Baptist."

"Once the Rapture is complete, the persons left behind will have another opportunity to repent, and that's where we come in. The Greenest Pasture delivers a digital message from the Saved to their damned loved ones. Our subscribers know that someone they love will reject the gift of Christ's blood—until it is too late."

I grew up with all of the religious code words and scare tactics, but I cringed anyway.

"I can see that you are truly devoid of faith, Declan. Only a person of your profound ignorance —no offense," Greg smiled, "can be trusted to remain on Earth and send these messages from our Raptured congregation."

"I get it; I'm the atheist waiting to press the Rapture button."

"Something like that. In the end, God's will is being done, even by an atheist. Isn't God amazing?"

"Did the last guy..."

"Yes. Stephen Patrick accepted Christ as his Lord and Savior last month, God bless him. He lost his job but gained eternity at the right hand of Christ."

"My good fortune it seems."

"Stephen Patrick's conversion reminded us that the great state of Texas is God's country. The board decided to move the operation to one of the few remaining regions dense with non-believers. I was tasked with finding a Systems Administrator who would be guaranteed to push the button. Can we count on you, Declan?"

"I am a devout non-believer, and neither you, nor an army of snake-handling televangelists will ever change that." I intended to remain a dirty heathen, collect my tidy salary, and wait for an apocalypse that was never coming.

"Declan," Greg rose to shake my hand, "welcome to The Greenest Pasture."

II

Jenny the Cat Bleacher was surprised. It felt good to tell her I was leaving. She asked about my new job because she thought she should, but I told her not to worry about it. I planned on paying for the rest of the month in a couple of days.

She smiled, "Oh, well thank you. It'll be weird for the attic to be empty again."

I started to climb the spiral staircase and didn't respond.

I moved my box and a half of belongings into suite 1204 early the following Sunday morning. The doorman let me into the suite, and as soon as I had set my box down, my phone buzzed.

"Declan, it's Greg."

"I figured. I'm getting myself moved in."

"So I see. Don't worry, your room is devoid of monitoring devices but the rest of the building is...well, no one will be stealing our doughnuts, eh?"

"Shouldn't you be at church, Greg?"

"I'm dropping by the office for a moment before I go. See you soon."

⋈

Greg stepped from the elevator in his Sunday best.

"Wow boss, looking sharp."

"Thank you, Declan. Are you settled in?"

"I am."

"Excellent. Stephen Patrick was a meticulous record keeper, and he canonized all procedures and processes prior to leaving. In his words you should be able to pick right up and run.

"Here are the physical keys to the shop and your passcard. Both the key and the passcard are necessary to lock the doors. If you lose these items, contact me immediately and maintain visual surveillance over the office."

"No problem, Greg. Are you turning me loose?"

"Yes, your confidence is contagious. I booked a flight for shortly after this morning's service at Bel Air Presbyterian. There is a very special young lady I want a chance to speak to before I return to Texas."

"Greg, you sly dog, you."

Greg smiled, "Well, we'll see won't we?"

⋈

I ended up in Pathos, but I waited until 5pm in case Greg was still watching. As I opened the door, bright daylight penetrated the tomb-like bar. The unwelcome sunshine served as a reminder that the world carried on just beyond the afternoon stupor.

I ordered a stout, and the bartender snapped his fingers, remembering something important. "Watch out for the guys on the corner. They're not real cops; they're worse. Anyway, my shift is over." I handed him a five dollar bill. "Thanks, be careful out there."

I shared the bar with one other patron. He had his head bowed toward a half-empty yellow beer. His gaunt cheeks, bony hands, and disheveled hair painted a portrait of dedicated self-destruction.

I heard the voice whisper over my shoulder again.

Goddamn church is getting obnoxious, Declan.

"How do you know my name?"

I don't know your name, Declan.

My barmate never lifted his head.

"Great, a ventriloquist and an asshole."

The bartender was talking about the men on the corner. They belong to the Civility Guard.

I ignored him. The new bartender said hello, but seemed not to notice the corpse whispering to me.

Being 'mad with drink' is a punishable offense.

"Look pal, as far as I can tell we're strangers. Let's keep it that way."

You hate pushy people. I am not a pushy person by nature, but you are being more stubborn than I had anticipated.

"I don't know what any of that means, but I'm here to celebrate being employed." I motioned to the new bartender, "A stout for myself, and another of whatever this gentleman likes." I turned back to the stranger. "Now, I've offered a gesture of goodwill. Please leave me be."

The new bartender sighed wearily. "It's just you and me cowboy, and I'm in the Program. You want that second drink now, or later?"

The strange man was still hunched over his yellow beer. How did the bartender not see him? I felt nauseated.

Don't throw up. This is the only place I can speak freely with you.

"I didn't ask for this. Whatever is happening is not okay with me..."

The man raised his forlorn eyes and nodded. I blinked, and he was gone.

I downed the stout and waved to the bartender, "Make the second a whiskey neat. Whatever you have that doesn't come from a plastic bottle."

Monday morning hurt. I drank long into the night trying to conjure the man, but he never returned. I felt like a bundle of mistakes, and the dehydration only gave my regret a physical dimension.

Not the best way to start a job, but I've failed harder without trying. I had hot coffee on my desk and all systems running through process logging in twenty minutes.

Greg texted —Back in God's country, amen. Thank you for being punctual. I trust you have everything you need, if not let me know. May God bless us all.

I replied —Glad you are home safe, and will do.

—Did you see that speech in Iowa last night? Man, I've never been this excited about a President. He really is of the People.

—Didn't see it.

—Good thing, our President has the power of persuasion.

If you're a brain dead moron, sure...

I had a lot of reading to do.

✄

After a few paychecks, I could finally afford to have lunch in the neighborhood, something other than tacos or a cheap sandwich—3/4 bread 1/4 meatcheesewhatever. I grabbed a short booth in the last hipster diner on Ivar Street. All of the businesses that came to the neighborhood via gentrification, were long gone. When it became clear that the impoverished and criminal were not leaving Hollywood without a fight, investors got spooked and sent their development money Downtown, where it's 3 cops to each citizen.

Every television was tuned to the President's favorite news outlet. It's hard to block it out, but you have to try. There aren't many true believers in Hollywood, which is why I stuck around, but local businesses kept the sainted news channel on twenty-four hours per day, like a great shrieking mouth.

Greg texted —Happy month-a-versary!

—Thanks! All is well.

—I know. How is your spiritual struggle?

—Non-existent.

—Amen.

The only waitress in the diner stood behind the bar with the only bartender and the host. They were staring blankly at the President, whose twisted face consumed the HD monitor hung above the horseshoe-shaped bar. Someone turned the volume up.

Folks...folks, look, a problem, yes. We have many of them, things that aren't right. So true...but now, people are speaking, with tongues, and lips, and voices. A wonderful thing to see, to taste, and hear. Because of this I cannot stand by, yes I have tears here folks, believe me. I cannot allow good god-fearing people to be abused. Across our waving nation of greatness...Yes, sea to ocean, to desert, patriots communing with groups of like-minded Americans, patriots like our own George Washington for instance. Fighting, and fighting *what is right, always. So, of course, we are federally funding these groups. What are they?" *offcamera whispering* "Yes, City Guard Posts. Guards, folks, Civility Guards I'm told. They're here to make you live a better life. Are they cops? Maybe, who cares? They care. About crime. And terrorists. About people determined to destroy the undestroyable love of Christ Jesus. Can't be destroyed, folks. Even Allah knows. These guards, crusaders really, will clean up our streets, keep an eye on those who bring harm, and mess with our way of life. The Liberals can't tread on us. No means no. Am I right? Folks... In the end, through me, mostly through me, God's will is being done.*

The bartender, "Does anyone know what that idiot is rambling about?"

The waitress, "He's drunk. He has to be."

The host, "He's talking about church police. Like, walking around calling people out for cussing and short skirts."

The waitress, "You have to be kidding."

The host, "They've been around for a long time. They used to stage large protests at the funerals of famous social activists. They think they are doing god's work. Most people ignore them, obviously they are whacked. But now, I mean look who our President is..."

The bartender, "Yeah, well, watch yourself. Saying shit like that will get you fired."

The host, "Fuck 'em. Silence is guilt."

The waitress, "Complicity. Silence is complicity."

The host, "Oh, guys, there's someone here."

The waitress walked toward me craning her neck to see the screen.

"Hey."

"Hello." I smiled but for naught. "Bacon and eggs, lots of coffee, and a double whiskey neat. Irish whiskey if you have it."

"Cool. Did you come here for the Emergency Text Party? It got canceled, you know."

"No. Just here for lunch. What's the Emergency Text Party?"

The waitress pointed to a poster in the doorway. "Protest of some sort. Against the President's emergency warning thing-a-ma-bob. Rumor has it someone squealed and the whole party had to go underground."

"I guess I'm a little behind on the times."

She walked toward the kitchen watching the screen intently.

Jenny the Cat Bleacher was waiting at the entrance to the Taft building when I returned.

"Finally." Her hand was frantically tapping out a cigarette. "You forgot to leave your new number and address. I remembered you said something about working here, so, yeah. I have mail for you." She reached into her handbag and produced several envelopes.

"Thanks, I appreciate that. I have the same number, I can't imagine why I didn't see your calls..." I opened the lobby door.

"Aren't you going to show me your new office?"

I smiled and closed the door behind me.

Mom's penmanship was improving, but more and more, she was speaking in someone else's voice. *My son, I know you don't get involved in politics, but there are dangerous people flooding into this country, taking good jobs from Americans like Robert, and trying to destroy our way of life. Our President is taking care of them. He is restoring our pride.* The fear of foreign invasion came from her news stories, perhaps my stepfather. *Sometimes you just have to go back to your heritage. You have to stand up for what the country means. I am sad about what is happening, but the President gives me hope.* Mom continued to hint at the big surprise I had in store; I couldn't decide if she was building tension or forgetting she had mentioned it. What was clear: she was gleefully preparing for war, and for someone in her condition, that was an unhealthy focus.

I walked to a nearby liquor store, and took home a bottle of Irish brown—breaking my cardinal rule: never drink at home, especially alone. The possibility of a conversation with the whispering man was good enough to keep me away from Pathos, and everywhere else had that abominable news station blaring.

As the elevator crept to a stop on the twelfth floor, my phone buzzed.

PRESIDENTIAL ALERT

THIS IS A TEST of the President's Communication Network. All is well, this is only a test. God bless our United State.

Everyone was looking at their phone. Some were bewildered—I could relate—some smirked, and some shook their heads in resignation. I pulled up my own news stories and was disappointed to find our President had sent every last American a text message, whether they liked it or not. They did not provide an opportunity to opt-out.

It was an absurd violation: soft but penetrating. Privacy is only a marketing term; it was simple to look the other way and blame our vulnerability on our need to connect. The reality was much darker, much harder to swallow.

—Did you get it? Another text, Mom this time.
—Yeah. Pretty creepy.
—*look of confusion emoticon*
—The Presidential text message, it's creepy.
—No. My letter.
—Yes. I'll write back tonight.
—You are a good son.

III

I decided to explain to Mom the millions of reasons she was wrong in long form rather than text message—wrong about politics, wrong about America, and wrong about our outlandish President. Maybe a little subtle chipping at the more ridiculous aspects of her newfound cult would bring her around. Mom had always been an obey first, ask questions later sort of American, but this felt like something different.

The letter I wrote asked if she'd considered the hardships of the people she demonized. I didn't go any further, I imagined her tearfully reading my response, forever stuck in that bed, and I became weak. I went on to talk about my new job and its intriguing secrecy. I knew she'd be impressed that her son was finally doing something productive —religiously positive— and to my discredit, I was desperate for any way to make her days less bleak.

I dropped the letter into the only post box I could find and headed up to the office. Greg called as soon as I crossed the threshold.

"Greg man, that's kind of creepy."

"We have a problem. This is not a phone conversation."

"Ok, I know how to reach you."

I spun up a VPN and began an encrypted conversation with Greg.

—A security breach was just detected. Per our team, a lethal injection attack placed executable code into the database. The next person that purchases a subscription will trigger a worm and replicate it throughout all connected devices.

Greg was relying on the information provided to him, otherwise he'd know it's called a SQL injection attack. —Sounds like they got in through the app, I know what to do on my end.

I set to work determining whether my system had been compromised. Everything was coming up clean and passing inspection. Three small clusters of commands flashed by in the log for database credentialing. I scrolled back and found what I was looking for.

—The system was not compromised, Greg. I'm happy to report that the foreign code was isolated, triggered reporting in the appropriate logs, and never engaged with the server processes or had an opportunity to replicate.

—That is a relief. Good job, Declan. Send your report through this encryption key and then wipe it from your hard drive.

—It's only really clean when it's been burned to ash.

—That won't be necessary Declan, you passed the test.

⋈

The strange man was sitting at the end of the bar in the dark. I decided to take the seat next to him. His hands looked fragile: spindly and wrapped 'round his pint glass, still not quite empty. Pathos had hired another bartender. Their turnover made gaining local status impossible.

I motioned to the current bartender and waited as she helped everyone else. I could feel my shadow waiting to speak. "What do you want from me?"

Want. That's very interesting, I haven't considered our situation from that perspective.

"Our situation is the prelude to a restraining order..."

You're not convinced I'm real, Declan. Let's not be coy.

"Fine. At least tell me your name..."

The man turned his head and did not answer. He had wasted away since our last encounter. His face was hollow, and his skin had greyed to the pallor of necrotic disease. Before thinking, I asked, "Are you ill?"

Sickness pervades and penetrates our every waking moment, Declan. You can feel the rampant, naked aggression as it foments ancient rifts. Those that cling to the past, stand headlong against the world to come.

"Everything seems to be changing. I'll give you that, but I've been alive too long to fall for all that *this is the end* doom and gloom."

Of course, and to what end should we concern ourselves with the end, anyway? There will be more bloodshed Declan, of that, we can all be assured. The time to dam the floods has passed, now is the time to choose a shore.

"Jersey Shore."

That was funny.

My phone buzzed, but it didn't matter. "What are you afraid is coming?" The thin man was gone. I checked my phone, Mom again. I dialed as I walked out onto Hollywood Boulevard.

"What's up old lady?"

"Old lady? If I weren't in a wheelchair..."

Mom laughed. It always felt a little better when she laughed.

"So how's the weather in Orlando?"

"Hot, very hot. But we have good AC. God has truly blessed us."

"No, Robert's military benefits have truly blessed you."

"True, but the Lord God is working harder every day, you can see it happening."

"Right, in the rosy cheeks of a child, and the morning dew on a velvety clover..."

"No," she laughed, "it's even better. Abortion will be illegal soon."

Her glee disturbed me. "Not without overturning federal law..."

"You should watch the news." Her speech came slowly. "The Supreme Court voted."

"Wait, Mom, that's not a good thing. Roe vs. Wade isn't about a medical procedure."

"But killing babies is a sin, and we've angered God enough. Our President finally put someone on the court that understands that."

"I thought that guy turned out to be some sort of frat boy date-rapist."

"No, that was a conspiracy by the Left, trying to destroy a good god-fearing conservative man."

It was my turn to laugh. "I didn't pay much attention, but I can guarantee that if your President nominated him, he's neither good nor god-fearing."

"It is part of a plan by the Left to..."

"Mom, do you know what The Left is?"

"Communists."

"Well, partly. Democrats are The Left too."

"They are worse than communists, they are American communists." Mom wasn't really able to raise her voice anymore, but she would have, right then.

"Democrats are definitely worse than communists, but for the same reasons Republicans are worse than communists."

"I don't like any of them. They're all crooked." —it was the most forward-thinking thing I had heard her say in years— "But I thank God and the Republican party for giving us our President. He will make sure that in the end, God's will is done."

"What did you say?"

"I don't like any of them. They all lie..."

"No, just now, it felt familiar."

"Hold on son."—My stepfather asked Mom about taking his fishing boat out for the weekend —"Sorry, Robert needed to ask me something."

"I heard. Fishin' eh? Are you going along?"

"No, the chair is too heavy for the boat. Besides, why would I want to go fishing?" She laughed again.

"Touché, but you'll be alone for a long time."

"Oh it's ok, I'm used to it," more laughter, but to my ears bitter. "Robert takes very good care of me. He even took extra shifts the past two weeks."

"Are you guys cool?"

"Well, we're having a little trouble this month."

"How much do you need?"

"Nine hundred."

"Don't worry about it, I'll transfer the money as soon as we get off the phone." It felt strange to be able to conjure up that kind of money.

"Thank you son, Robert and I appreciate it."

"It's no problem. How did you guys get messed up for nine hundred bucks?"

"Oh, it was just a mistake. I have a subscription and there was an error. They charged my account twice."

"Are they going to fix it?"

"Yes. I have already called them. Our next month will be free." Mom giggled, proud of the accommodation.

"Well, it's not really free since you have already paid for it. And to make you wait instead of refunding the money, sounds shady to me."

"It's ok, I have a successful son who can help me."

"If you didn't, you'd be in trouble."

"That's true. I love you."

"I love you too, Momma. I need to jump off the phone..."

"Ok, thanks for calling me back. God bless..."

You are a good son.

The whispering man returned.

We sat in silence until Pathos closed its doors.

✂

Sleep was impossible. I wandered the office, fixed coffee, and smoked on the fire escape as the sun rose over south Vine Street. I tried to imagine the coming day as a reminder of Mom's benevolent god, as if the nourishment of the planet was ultimately god's will.

That was what I had heard, *god's will*. Mom said it, Greg said it, and above all, their Dear Leader said it. I rushed to my computer and scanned the offending code from the prior night's test. Hackers are humans and they can't fight their natural tendency toward failure. To find that failure, you just have to be able to see everything at once.

The attacker knew all about my system, so I decided to start with the entry point. I needed to see what, if anything, looked like untoward processes. I was able to isolate seven functions that failed to execute. Buried within a long string, I found the seven-digit serial number for the seventh encryption code on the list from Greg.

The attack was recycled: either copied from a better coder, or previously deployed, but the work was sloppy: my overseer had forgotten to remove his bridge back into the main system. Since he never really left the home network, the escape door lay dormant and unused.

Being underestimated by my employer's spies gave me the advantage, and the developing web of ominous intentions made it impossible for me to stay out. I wouldn't last long once I got inside, but if I could sneak a peek of what they were hiding, I'd get a better picture of who I was working for.

My guess about the encryption code proved correct. I was in with no hassle, and as far as I could tell, I wasn't setting off any alarms, so to speak. As I combed through directory listings I couldn't shake the feeling that all of this was a little too easy. Sure, I had a key to the door, but the only person authorized to use that key was verifiably in Texas. It was like something more important was sucking up all the attention.

The directories were a series of individual databases, each containing descriptions in a company lexicon, and what appeared to be digital coordinates for groups of data. The Greenest Pasture only existed on my side of the fence, which meant that we were feeding data into whatever was behind these databases. Encryption codes six and three, used in combination, opened the pathway from my little World into the larger Universe.

She was there, my Mom. I was in there as well, listed as the damned. The gift she had beamed about was her raptured message to me:

My poor lost son, I am sad about what is happening, but I am at peace because I know that in the end, God's will is being done.

I wasn't shocked, but my eyes filled with tears.

IV

I kept to chain restaurants, bustling plazas, and busy coffee shops—anywhere with a tv—until the tingling ends of my nerves numbed. The din of narcotized Presidential pronouncements faded far left of field and I sat there, day after day tending to my legion of parked condescending missives.

I tried hard to think of the money I was making instead of the vile undercurrent of hypocrisy I was shoring up. The subscriptions ranged from one hundred dollars per month for a standard *Wish you were here*, to the deluxe soul-crushing $1000 guilt subscription which laid out in great personal detail, every last thing your Raptured loved one thought you had done to deserve eternal hellfire.

I tried hard to think about the hope, deluded as it is, that belief gives to those hungry to judge. Most people had their minds tampered with at a young age, and it's hard for anyone to walk back that foundation. I can testify.

We are receiving new reports that an Associate Justice of the Supreme Court is in critical condition at an undisclosed location. It appears to have been a failed assassination. The DC Metro Police have no suspects, and at this time claim they have no leads. The Justice's spokesperson just gave a press statement over the phone.

...She was attacked in broad daylight, by persons who were intimately aware of her movements. Just like all of her peers before her. We cannot pretend that these systematic murders are a coincidence. We cannot remain silent when the media won't even say her name...

We all wish the Associate Justice a very speedy recovery. With only one Justice remaining, the President could very well remake the entire court in his image within the year. We live in very exciting times, right Sarah?

"Wait," the news story cut through, "when did that happen? They replaced eight Supreme Court Judges?"

"You got me buddy, who cares? Bunch of criminals anyway. You need a refill or what?" The bartender assumed, correctly, that I had just pulled out of a drunken haze.

"No, I'm good. I'm being serious, that's never happened before. Not in this country."

"What the hell do you know? No one gives a shit what you think unless you are a job-provider. We finally have a government that understands us."

"I feel like I know more, it's just all jumbled..."

"Here's the thing, if you don't like it, you can move to another country, problem solved."

I couldn't believe people still said things like that. I tipped poorly and left.

As I stumbled down Selma Avenue my phone buzzed again. I was in no shape to talk to anyone, it would have to wait. I made it to Pathos right before the evening crowd intensified and pulled up a stool near the end of the bar. I ordered a glass of water and sat in the dark, refusing to drink until the sick man appeared.

You are already drunk Declan, what are you trying to prove?

"That I still have some control."

The man whispered but would not appear. *Control. That's a very loaded word. You should check your text messages.*

"No thanks. Probably..."

It's not your mom.

"Ah, there you are." I looked the dying man in the eye, and his flesh hung tenuously from his skull. When I turned to ignore him, his cast reflection behind the bar was skeletal.

You should check your text messages.

8pm

PRESIDENTIAL ALERT
We call upon our people to express their Faith through prayer. This concludes your day of Worship. God bless our United State.

The alert comes three times a day, if you're into that sort of thing.

"For the record, I'm not."

Doesn't matter, does it? You get the message from El Presidente just like the rest of the morons.

"I'm pretty sure someone will tie this up in court. You can't just..."

Which court Declan? There aren't any left.

"They can send me messages about gods and godlike things until they are blue in the face. You're right, it doesn't matter."

Here's a thought. Maybe you're right, and there is no god. Maybe there's only an agreement to keep that a secret. Secrets have always had supernatural power.

"The Congress hasn't presented legislation in years, they just provide legal cover for the President's Executive Orders." I wasn't sure how I knew that, or why I said it.

Look around Declan, this is our world now. It's not coming, it's been here for a long time. Your apathy never protected you.

"My apathy? I'm not responsible for this..."

But you are Declan, responsible for every encroaching inch, each creeping schism you ignored because it did not affect your life. None of that matters now. What else did you see while you were inside the system, Declan?

"My mom..."

...Is a racist little troll. What else Declan? What were you trying to forget?

Her ugliness had been enough, and the realization that as I apologized for her cruel beliefs, I had only stacked brick and mortar against her Wall.

"It's an incredible eye."

Yes.

"They are watching at all times."

Yes.

"Labeling us unCivil when we think."

Yes. Your little pity party about dear old Mom is complicity.

"I can't bear to lose her, or this job."

Why do you think they hired you? Greg knows you're weak, he knows your weaknesses. You were cheap to dazzle, and cheap to maintain. A little funny business with dear old Mom's records brought you to heel, reminded you of your responsibilities, without lifting a finger.

The dying man's flesh had fallen completely away. To his audience of one, he presented only his raw core, nothing but hollow clacking bones devoid of sinew, devoid of mass.

"Then it doesn't matter what I do."

It never has.

"I should look after myself."

Yes.

⚥

The vast universe beyond the flagging databases was a churning cauldron. Data sets grew and evaporated like bricks in a massive breathing barrier. By freeing the data from structure, the system could devour information with reckless abandon and maximize storage potential. No thought was given to what is, or is not, important. The great eye's mission was only to collect and accuse.

I wrote a short, three-part script and introduced it into the main system via USB thumb drive. I waved to the cameras in the server room before locking the doors to the suite. The elegant—if I do say so myself—lines of code corrupted the flagging databases and rendered the massive stockpile of personal data a seething, chaotic mass, impossible to detangle. Before self-destructing, so to speak, the attack sent the paid-for messages of condemnation to the damned, en masse.

⚥

My actions were redemptive kindling
amidst a firestorm.
I should have gone farther,
but it was the last chance I got.

Forecasting

I was expected in Westlake Village by 9PM and I assumed that being late was some sort of deal breaker. I splashed a little aftershave on as I left the office and headed north on Argyle to the 101.

Laura slipped me her phone number on Wednesday. She works out in Los Angeles on Wednesdays and Fridays...lucky me. She was definitely "old money" and exactly the kind of person that led me to new clients.

Los Angeles faded into the dark night as I mounted and descended the rolling hills leading to Westlake Village, a strange oasis in hell. Just over the rise, Malibu was in flames, burning to the ground—one ill-conceived private estate after another. It had been burning for four days, a catastrophe for some, a miracle for me.

The restaurant was a beautiful spot, a good-looking rip-off of Frank Lloyd Wright with sporadic levels of horizontal lines splintered in green glass, coarse in texture. Semi-transparent walls blurred all sight, often dividing and subdividing the space into isolated sections—mesmerizing and unnerving.

I scanned the room and found her sitting near the end of the L-shaped bar, hidden from view, in premeditated privacy. She looked up as I made the corner and I saw her adjust in her seat. Her lips were wrapped around a straw planted deeply in a light emerald drink.

She waved for the bartender as I drank in her powdered, perfect facade. She was lovely. Exquisite eyes, shining and clear. Mirrors of light set against a sharp nose and pouting lips. Her skin was radiant, free from the friction of struggle.

I removed my jacket and hung it over my chair, and the bartender asked if we needed anything.

"Yes, would you like anything, darling?" She looked like she had already had a few, but it didn't hurt to ask.

"Yes, another mojito please."

"Mojito and a Sapphire and tonic. Thank you."

"So, Laura...it's very good to see you."

"MMM, it's good to see you too."

"Have you been waiting long?"

"I just sat down, ordered a drink and then...well, then you happened." She smiled, pressing her palm against my thigh and reaching for the rest of her drink. "What are you doing this weekend?" Laura asked.

"That depends."

As the bartender set her drink down she retreated, looking at him out of the corner of her eye. Laura already had plan b in place...my kind of gal.

We made our way through some extremely painful small talk and I realized that the only interest she had was in my work. Whatever did I do? I was certainly wearing a very nice suit for a date with *little old me*.

"I provide a specialized service to investors."

"Keep going..."

"Investors approach me about my forecasts." She was moving very close to me. I had my back to the bartender, but I had no doubt that her occasional side glance over my shoulder was to warn him to stay away, or to see if he was watching.

"So...forecasts? Hmmm, let me guess, stockbroker, or insurance..."

"Well, more like generalized assumptions about the viability of high profile and rapid return properties."

"What do you mean, rapid return?"

"Well, rapid as in fast, and return as in insurance, land, private property, et cetera. Irreplaceable valuables are a big hit with my customers."

I may as well have been shouting at a wall, her mind was attached to her hands and her hands were invariably attached to me and her drink.

"They like to fill their homes with priceless heirlooms and works of art. Truth be told, we've found some sneaking valuables out the side to cheat the insurance, but these are small time players and we weed them out accordingly. You cannot completely stop attempts to cheat the system, but who cares? It works for the majority of people and that is what is important."

"I still don't get it, what are you forecasting?"

"Major catastrophes. Do you know what is happening just over the hill in Malibu right now?

"Um..." She tightened her grip on my leg, seeking to be freed from my on the spot current events quiz.

"Malibu is on fire."

"Right. So..."

"So this happens every few years. 2003 was almost identical. Malibu burned, like kindling. In the 1400s people paying attention knew that this place was a firestorm waiting to happen. Seems that the combination of chaparral brush and high winds makes the whole region virtually impossible to protect from fire. By burning the brush, fresher, water-laden brush regrows, minimizing the potential destruction. According to monastery records Spanish conquerors forced the indigenous people living in and around Malibu Canyon to cease their yearly burning off of brush. With construction and development of the land, that brush is allowed to grow and dry out, sometimes for years or decades, until it finally goes up in flames."

"Why would people live in Malibu?"

"That's a damn good question. It was privately held land for most of its history, including a time when it had armed fence posts guarded by Rhoda May Rindge. Lawsuits and diminishing wealth forced her to sell off pieces to high paying developers and friends. Piece by piece Malibu was subdivided and turned into a resort town. The development companies have since benefited from placing residences as far into the canyon as legally (and sometimes extra-legally) possible."

"How big are the bets?"

"The ante is in the high nine digits, and I never lose."

"But that's ridiculous...um...isn't it?"

"It guarantees that undesirables are unable to participate. Back in the 1980s some douche from Deloitte and Touche got a bright idea...

"Look, all I'm saying is that if you want to get rid of all of this evidence, I have an idea."
"I'm not sure I want to hear this."
"Trust me, you do..."

"His client needed to remove $30 million worth of taxable income from his books, in a hurry. Three years would be too long. Two would be pushing it.

He needed something airtight because he was under investigation for securities fraud...

"This is the plan. We buy a nice, large plot of land in Malibu Canyon, in January. By November the next year, we have a three story, fifteen room estate erected. Fill it with every valuable piece of furniture, stock, and evidence. Then, you declare publicly that you are planning on taking a break from public life and want your retreat to be overlooking the beautiful city of Malibu.

"Okay, it sounds nice, but the feds will be all over me.

"What happens every 2-3 years in Malibu?"

"The number of plastic surgery disasters increases."

"Firestorms. I say we open a new market, FORECASTS LLC."

"The clients secure an airtight insurance policy, it's like loaning the bank nine figures for 2 years. They pay off on it, but you lose all of that equity, it burns, and in your name it can be disappeared."

"What do you get out of it?"

"That depends on the client."

"What's the best you've pulled down?"

"I'm not at liberty to discuss it. Let's just say I ended up with a position of power that I did not deserve. Money isn't always the goal."

"Well, it should be."

"Think about it, if you spend $300 million on a dream getaway everyone will understand the excess. You're basically pouring money into something that is a sedentary, and relatively permanent manifestation. All kinds of things go wrong and all kinds of extra money needs to be poured in periodically, including money paid out to city and state officials...

"While you're at it you end up paying out a bunch of contractors and no one digs deep enough to see that you are simply paying your constituents, or your cronies. It's money laundering, but it's inconspicuous, wretchedly decadent, and invites the grandest of excesses. Each year the clients race to build larger, more bacchanal, orgiastic gardens of Eden only to watch them set aflame one, two, five years into the future. Each year they heap on more adornment and prepare for the queen mother of short-term investments.

"If you luck into a five year cycle (and that's why they call it forecasting) you push to join city councils, get elected, and start manipulating privatization of local functions until you are able to cash in on your *distress* at your *perfect paradise* being *burned to a beautiful cinder.* Thereby capturing the governor's primary by a hairline victory as a moderate from Malibu...see?

"A lot of people used this natural phenomenon to profit and they were only able to do it by hiding what was in plain sight, bait and switch. There are very subtle allusions to very bad years in the past, the further in the past the better. Local news plays up the turmoil and distress of the poor rich people as their pyres to piety are scorched beyond recognition, untold millions that could have gone anywhere other than up in flames."

Her face scrunched up in feigned disgust. Her lips curled malignantly upward as she asked calmly..."Like where?"

"Anywhere it could have helped someone, anyone."

I'd gone too far. Her eyes dropped from mine and her smile evened. Laura's face smoothed as if gently containing a long endured prejudice.

"But why would they do that? It's their money isn't it?"

"Yes it is, and it is their prerogative to do with it as they please."

Her face brightened again and she purred something blasphemous in my ear about the patio and smoking.

I stood and held out my arm for her to take. She stumbled a little and I guided her to the patio.

We were one of three couples in the rather large restaurant. We took a seat beneath a heat lamp on a very comfortable outdoor sofa. The black sky was dotted by brilliant white pinpricks of ancient light. The soft green glow from the restaurant muzzled the bright flames in the nearby fire pit and placed a haze of cool over the patio. As we smoked she wrapped her leg around mine and I placed my open hand around her thigh.

"So how does a nice boy like you get involved in a business like that?"

"It was a sound investment, mother nature took care of the odds, and people started to get creative with it. All over the country, any disaster prone area has its own forecasting pool. After playing the game for a couple of years, I realized I had a knack for picking winners.

"Malibu is actually the elite playing field in forecasting...which is why I can wear an 8000$ suit to see *little old you*."

Laura looked dreamily and drunkenly into my eyes. She wrapped her wrists around my neck and pulled herself onto my lap.

"Let's get out of here..."

"Yes, I believe it is time we departed."

Laura mistakenly walked down the handicap ramp, turned, and had to steady herself against the bar. I instinctively reached out to help and ended up laughing behind her with one hand on her hip and one on the rail.

She lingered, concentrating and then smiled.

"So I bet you have a nice laaaaaarge place," her tongue curled and vibrated over the sentence.

"No, I am a humble man. I have a tiny cottage in North Hollywood."

"Oh. Well, I figured you got a larger cut than that." She seemed suddenly distressed, as if she had made a grave error.

"I am paid handsomely, but I don't devote it completely to excess."

"Well, my father would never trust a consultant living in a hobo shack."

"What kind of work does your father do?"

"No one in my family has *worked* for hundreds of years. He buys churches, the rest is very very boring."

"You should introduce me. I guarantee he'd see things my way." I kissed her neck softly while I dropped a business card with a tiny microphone in her purse and she gripped my hair.

"You're weird! So which car is yours? No man can resist a beautiful car...wait, let me guess..."

"Silver Dodge Neon."

"That's hilarious, stop fucking with me, I'm trying to decide if I should leave my car here!"

"I'm serious. there she is."

"Um, it was nice to meet you, I think I should be going though."

In an instant it had turned from fine whipping cream into curds, admonished by the implements of status. As California continued to burn, I had a feeling my card would find its way to her father and I'd get the information I needed. I don't drive a Dodge Neon, but I knew it would help her make the right decision.

Athens Diptych II

Almost

On the night Evelynn Holyoake was born, dense thunder clouds threatened to obscure the star-addled summer sky.

"Here it is, 310 Clover. Pull around the side, there's a good view of the backyard."

"Looks like a postcard. This guy's a family man now?"

"Yeah, he's been busy. Got a pretty wife, kid on the way. He'll back down if he has any sense. God willing."

"They never do."

"Bahnsen was very specific. He has a few more hours to call in, we have to wait."

"He won't call in, let's just take care of it now."

"No. We're keeping eyes on him until the deadline. We have our orders."

☒

Sitting across from Fatima less than a week ago, Declan combed his hair back with a sigh. "I need this deal to go through. I dragged Adeline to this podunk town and now we're trapped."

Fatima sat forward. "It doesn't matter what we want. Keith pulled out, there's no deal."

"There's a deal if we say there is. It's a con. The point is we don't have what we offer."

"But we need to have it for as long as they are checking. You're desperate Declan, you need to cool it."

"I don't want my kid born in this dump. I need out, and I need out now."

"No suicide missions, remember?"

"I remember." Declan stood. "I need to pick the Mom-to-be up from the baby shower."

"How's everything going?"

"So far, so good. The baby'll be here any day now." Declan rapped a wood rail thrice. "We need to leave, and soon."

⚔

Adeline called from the living room, "Honey, did you move the laptop charger?"

"Um. Yes, it's in here." Declan closed his laptop and walked the charger to his wife. Adeline was sitting, Buddha-like, in the glow of her laptop screen. "You should sleep once in a while. You're pregnant and all."

"I should," Adeline smiled sweetly and kissed her concerned husband. "And I will, as soon as I wrap up this proposal. I only need a few more days and they'll be begging to make me an offer."

"Back to Los Angeles."

"Back to our home."

Declan fumbled in his pockets.

"I don't regret coming to Georgia," Adeline offered, "it's just time to go."

Rachel finished dressing while the sun punished the Vegas valley. *Ok now, you've got this. Yesterday was pretty bad but you got through it. Today will be no worse and you will get through it too.* Rachel's long white cigarette had gone out while she finished her eyes. She relit the ashen tip and walked into the living room. There was a similarly half-smoked and ashen cigarette on the coffee table, dining room table, and kitchen counter. The oven clock read 6:50am so she had time for another half-smoke and a soda before her commute. Ten short years ago Rachel could drive from one side of Vegas to the other in 20 minutes, now she had to leave an hour early just to get half that far.

"Hey, Sis."

"Hey you, how's it going?"

Rachel lit a cigarette. "Great, I'm driving to work and need a little company. Is that ok?"

"Of course, thanks for calling me."

Rachel's sister Shirley lived in their home town. Rachel was trying to convince her to leave the Lone Star State and come out to Nevada. Shirley's health had been better, and frankly, Rachel's had been too. They were the only remaining sisters from a family of nine. The brothers were stubborn, like their father, and were best avoided.

"So when you movin' out here, girl? Ain't gettin' any cheaper," Rachel laughed.

"Well, I wanted to talk to you about that. I was thinkin'," Shirley chose her words carefully, "I know you're not really as happy as you say you are. I think what you need is a fresh start. We have a lot of jobs down here, and you know you're a Texas girl when it comes down to it."

"I can't leave him yet. I'm close, Sis, but I need to save a little more money."

"Save it here. I can't help but feel like somethin' needs to happen. And soon."

"I feel it too. At least I have a job, girl. My dang meeting with the health insurance rep. got pushed til Friday."

"What? That's ridiculous."

"I know, I've been getting woozy spells and the headaches are still popping up here and there. But at least I'll have insurance by week's end. "

"Your own insurance."

"Exactly. Ow. Oh, hey Sis?"

"Yeah, you okay?"

"I just got a really bad migraine all of a sudden and my vision is a little...weird..."

"Sis, pull over just in case, ok?"

"..."

"Sis?"

⚔

Declan's section lead hovered a moment before tapping him on the shoulder.

Declan quickly minimized his work screen and pulled off his headphones. "What?"

"What are you working on?"

"Is that why you're here?"

"No. Your wife called while you were at lunch. Something about your cell not answering."

Declan checked his desk; his phone was dead. "Thanks, anything else?"

"Nope." the co-worker smirked.

Declan purged the directory before shutting his computer down. He figured out another way to put Fatima's plan in motion, solo and under the radar, but he had to hurry. Bahnsen knew where to find him now.

"Dan."

"Yup."

"My phone's dead and the wife called, mind if I use your..."

"Nope."

Fucking voicemail. "Hey gorgeous, it's me. Calling from Dan's phone. I'm charging my phone, call me back. Love 'ya."

✄

When it finally charged, Declan's phone was alight with text messages and missed calls from hospital staff. The baby was arriving.

When he got to Athens Regional Hospital, Adeline was holding a silent baby girl in her arms. A nurse handed him clothing to change into and

Declan could not contain his excitement. Adeline cried out and the delivery room became a blur of blue clothing as they whisked mother and daughter to an operating room.

Declan was made to wait hours into the night before he was summoned. He stood at the door to the NICU and, as instructed, peered into the convex security eye. Eventually a buzzer announced that the door was unlocked. The walkways of the NICU were dark and silent. Rows of plastic cases awry with wires and tubes lined the corridor. Meek beeps and whirs surfaced from the silence.

He heard Adeline weeping before he saw her, crumpled in a formed plastic chair. Her knees were drawn to her chin and her hair was wet with tears. Declan embraced her, which only made her weep more violently.

"What happened? Where's the baby?"

Adeline pointed weakly to a plastic case against the far wall. Their child lay writhing inside, unable to communicate her agony, tiny hands groping the air for comfort.

"She's dying. I overheard." Adeline continued to stare at the floor.

"I don't understand."

"They don't know for sure what it is." Adeline looked for Declan's eyes but they were trained on the newborn. "Her organs are shutting down; failing is the word they used."

"She's not dying, she's going to pull through. This is not your fault, don't blame..."

"Don't. Not now. Please."

"Ok. I'm sorry."

☒

The hospital grudgingly agreed to let Adeline sleep in the NICU, but put their foot down when it came to two parents, even called the cops. Declan walked the winding mile home to 310 Clover Street and was casually feasted upon by a legion of mosquitoes as dusk settled into sunset. The house was dark and his truck was in the driveway. Adeline didn't understand why he kept the truck; they walked everywhere, but he needed a means of escape to feel safe.

Declan had planned to be halfway to Memphis with Adeline by sunset; the baby arriving made that impossible. In a few minutes the wrong people would find out about Declan's plan, and Fatima was now in great danger. He could get in the truck, spring Adeline and the child, and just drive west. They'd make it; they'd always made it somehow before.

He flipped on lights in every room of the house searching for cigarettes. A small box popped up on his phone as he sat down on the back steps. A message from Aunt Shirley: *Rachel passed this morning. Please, call me as soon as you can.*

Declan dropped his phone and watched it succumb to a slowly building rain.

And Don't Look Back

The NICU was beset with thunderclaps and flashes of dense light. The Nurse did not know the woman's name—just a rude mother grabbing her arm while she was delivering steroids to bed twenty-six.

"Does this exit lead to the parking lot?"

"Yes, near the bus shelter."

The woman brushed past the Nurse and rushed to the door with her phone to her ear. "Ok. Please tell me, where is he?"

Her baby began to cry softly. The Nurse approached the child and tried to soothe her. She lay in a plastic box fighting for her life; the parents hadn't even bothered to name her. When the baby fell back to sleep the Nurse completed her errand.

⚔

"Has anyone seen her parents?"

Sylvia scolded, "Annabelle, it's only been a few days..."

"Get out of here, the mom is off her rocker and dad's nowhere to be found."

The Nurse asked, "What happens to kids like that? I mean kids who are going to need a lot of help?"

"Hey, New Girl jumped in. Welcome to the conversation, West Coast." Annabelle socked the Nurse on the shoulder. "Sylvia's the resident expert."

Sylvia smoothed her uniform. "Well, it's not a black and white process..."

Annabelle smirked. "That's just something bosses say..."

"Well, I'm saying it too. It can be determined by a lot of variables."

The Nurse pressed. "What about negligent parents?"

"Well," Sylvia smiled tiredly at the Nurse, "that would kind of disqualify most of the community we serve."

"So that's why it's complicated? Tolerance has guidelines?"

"Tolerance is based on culture, and in this particular culture, unless you can prove in court that a child is in danger, the State sides with family."

"White families." Annabelle added.

"Unfortunately, yes."

The Nurse wondered what would constitute danger if those parents didn't. Dangerous or not, the Nurse never saw them again.

⚔

"...Bed seven is doing well, considering, but she's got a lifetime of medical problems to contend with. Her parents are still missing in action, so we, the nurses, nicknamed her Evelynn. Her little neighbor Lee is rapidly declining, unfortunately. Dr. Khohaktar wants us to make the parents as comfortable as possible, it may only be a matter of days for Lee."

"Thank you, Annabelle. Unless anyone has something to add, we are adjourned..." Head Nurse Benson swept the room with her eyes.

"Evelynn's parents aren't coming back." The Nurse commented.

"We are aware. The proper documentation has been filed, nurse. Legally, there isn't much we can do but wait."

"What about morally? We're sending that child to her death. And we know it."

"We have our orders, like everybody else, and that little girl is on her way to becoming a ward of the state of Georgia. There's nothing you, I, or the sweet baby Jesus can do."

"So we give up..."

"That will be all, nurse."

"Yes, nurse Benson."

"Back to work, please."

Annabelle caught up with the Nurse. "What are you gettin' at, city girl?"

"What? Nothing. I know I got a little heated, but damn it, that little girl deserves..."

"A legit start in life? Yeah, they all do. You know who gets it? Lee. Not Evelynn. Not ever Evelynn. And that is the way it is, West Coast."

"We can't just give up on her."

Sylvia caught up. "You planning on taking her home with you? Save her, maybe? There'll be a wall of Clarke County Sheriff's deputies that say otherwise. This is a bad situation, we're surrounded by bad situations in the NICU. If you can't muscle up, you might want to focus on older patients."

Annabelle and Sylvia knew what the Nurse was going through, but time heals all wounds, and strips rebellion of its power. Without armor, without a beleaguered sense of duty, the Nurse didn't stand a chance.

Annabelle put her hand warmly on the Nurse's back. "Sylvia's just a savage, don't listen to her. If you ever stop caring about what happens to these precious little angels, you walk out that door and don't look back, you hear?"

The Nurse smiled. "Loud and clear."

⚔

Graveyard shift was off limits to parents, but as long as the Nurse was on duty, Lee's mom was allowed to stay. And she stayed, day and night, by her child's side. Evelynn's call button lit up. Annabelle was slowly pecking her way through some record entries.

"That's weird. Someone pushed Evelynn's button, you want me to take over the paperwork?"

"Hell no, I'm not getting any faster at this by giving it to you."

"Ok. I'll be back."

The Nurse began the long walk through the silent NICU. The new shine of the floors at 4am was penetrating. A small cry rose from the din of monitors.

"Nurse, nurse, please help."

The Nurse began running; Lee's mother was standing outside of Evelynn's curtain.

"She began to fuss, and then she cried out once and seemed to be choking. The muffled sound, I'm sorry, I know I'm not supposed to...but she looks so much like Lee, I couldn't...is she, ok?"

The Nurse ran through the vitals, Evelynn's O2 levels were low, but all else was normal. "I think our little buddy will be ok."

"Are you sure? She sounded so desperate. I'm sorry, she just looks so much like...I was rushing to get you before I knew what I was doing."

"I wish more people cared as much as you do." The Nurse smiled.

"Is it that bad?"

"Is what, *that bad*?"

"The parents here. I mean. I don't see very many parents on a regular basis."

The Nurse turned her head. Her throat tightened. "It's a crime." A moment of weakness. "But we have to do our best for the children in all situations." A moment of strength, of apathy.

"How do you...is it hard?"

"Extremely."

Lee's mother touched the Nurse's shoulder. "You are a stronger woman than I am. I wouldn't last a day."

The Nurse wanted to tell Lee's mother that she was not going to make it home. She wanted her to understand the futility of Lee's situation, that her daughter would not slip away in her sleep, that she would suffer. The mother's kindness could not save her, but it could save someone else.

"What happens? When they don't make it?" Lee's mother looked down on Evelynn, hoping to hide that she was asking about her own daughter.

"They make it." The Nurse smiled and placed her hand on the mother's.

"Thank you. Will this little girl be adopted?"

"I hope so. I'm not inclined to send her home." The Nurse paused. "I'm sorry, that was inappropriate."

"Even so, I appreciate your honesty. There's not a lot of honesty around here. I should get something to eat."

"Take your time, Lee is in good hands."

Lee's mother began to cry and smiled away the first tears.

⚔

"Are you ok, West Coast?"

"Yeah. I think so."

"You should take a couple days off. Why not?" Sylvia offered.

"Yeah, why not?" Annabelle chimed in.

"I said I'm ok."

"You said you think you're ok. That's not..."

"Sylvia, Annabelle, I am ok. Ok?"

"Ok."

Annabelle wasn't buying it. "Whatever, West Coast. You're the one walking around here talking about justice, and look what happened. Little Evelynn, who no one cared about, except you, up and died in the middle of the night. An' you mean to tell me you aren't damaged? Say it again..."

"Justice is subjective. We did all we could for Evelynn. I shake my fist at whatever deity will listen, but she's dead. Ok? And she was dead if she left here, so it's not my justice, but it's somebody's justice."

Sylvia frowned. To become too cold was also not the way. "You're right, she had nowhere to go, but you already knew that."

The Nurse averted her eyes. "None of it matters. I'm leaving today. My husband got a job offer."

"You're running."

"Maybe. This place makes no sense to me. The Sheriff shows up when someone tries to help but won't show up when the parents refuse to."

"It's the same no matter where you go. You are just more likely to recognize the faces 'round here."

The Nurse never said goodbye.

⚔

Annabelle found a handwritten message in the back of the Nurse's old desk as she cleaned it out. "Sylvia, did you get this message about a Sheriff's Deputy asking for a call back? Uh oh, it's a few days old..."

"Yes. They sent a Deputy over to tell us about Evelynn's parents."

"Wait, they found them?" Annabelle grabbed Sylvia's arm.

"Dead."

"Oh no..."

"The husband disappeared for three days after the baby came. The police found him at the house, full of bullet holes. When they called to inform the mother, she walked right into oncoming traffic."

The Interior

The bright light never ceased. As the young man approached it, the light began to speak. Vulgarities to the young man's ears, but that was his society's doing. The light was pregnant with imagery, by leaps and bounds the best of the best and no less. The young man could feel the images; tendrils of lust stealing his breath.

The light explained that these feelings could be his; he deserved to own them. *What you desire defines you. What you desire sets you free. The Interior sets you free.*

With mention of The Interior, the spell was broken. The young man was well-informed about the perils of The Interior and their wantonness. But it felt so real. Terror so sublime that it was invigorating. He returned to his work station and completed his duties.

When the young man returned to the bright light, it had dimmed. He succumbed to the light's power, but it no longer satisfied him.

There is more, the bright light lulled. *I can show you more.*

⚔

The young man left at dawn and arrived at the border by midday. The ruling parties of The Interior insisted on cataloging all border-crossings for future reference. Hundreds of his neighbors clambered for the attention of the representatives—young, vibrant emissaries from The Interior.

By nightfall the young man passed into a foreign land. The walls, streets, people, and the sky itself, were awash in words and images—large, epic murals of pleasure and naught else. Feelings were commandments and the proselytizers were their valiant champions. The young man entered a tall building and approached a woman in a cage.

Hello, I've just arrived. Where do I apply for lodging?

Great, another one. You freaks can't stay here for free. It's 20,000 Nadir a night. If you fuck anything up, it'll cost 'ya a lot more.

I don't have currency, it is not our way. But I am not a freak, I am an upstanding...

If you don't have Nadir, get the hell out of here.

I will just need one night, and I can repay you. I'm certain to be a part of the Larger Dream now that I am here.

Harold, the woman called to the back of her cage. *We've got a nutjob out here that is refusing to pay. Just skipped the border without any Nadir.*

Before the young man could react, Harold emerged from a doorway and struck him against the skull. Harold repeatedly bludgeoned the young man's face and arms until he stumbled onto the street. Harold did not give chase.

A citizen wearing a vivid indigo cloak stopped to help the young man up. The stranger's skin and ringed fingers seemed to shine.

You must be new here.

Yes. I'm sure that's obvious.

I'm Maya. Maya brushed off the young man's clothing. *What do people call you?*

I've never used a name.

Oh, you're really new. I'll call you Clay for now.

I don't care what you call me. I need to find work.

Come with me, Clay. I can show you more.

The young man paused. He'd heard that before.

Maya winked, *You aren't scared of having a good time are you?*

⚸

The crowded, sticky streets ceded to a large empty lot. Long dead Black Birch formed a sinister forest that was hard to see for the trees. Masses of people moved in and out of the lot and amongst the skeletal birch, small tents, and lean-to shelters.

Maya led the young man through the throngs of mesmerized humans and stopped at a dirty grey tent scrawled with bizarre symbols in thick red paint across the entrance. *Are you ready, Clay?*

Ready for what?

Maya smiled and opened the tent's flaps, *Welcome to The Interior.*

Great screens choked the tent with calming light. The young man felt more at ease, more balanced, wiser. He took a seat on the soft cushions lining the center of the tent. From the outside, one would never know that such beauty and light was contained in the filthy little tent. The young man closed his eyes and the light began to speak.

You are chosen. This is all for you. This is all because of you. Life is an illusion that must be navigated carefully and with little remorse. You are destined to transcend, if you put in the work. Visions of otherworldly beauty and perfection clouded the young man's eyes and his heart began to race. *Yes, you have the right to feel like this. To be in touch with domination. You will one day be like us. It is within your power.*

The voice ceased and the young man felt a great and wrenching pain, an unbearable longing. Though Maya had long since disappeared, the young man waited for the voice to return. When he emerged from the tent, three days had passed. Beyond the light of the tent, the young man was overwhelmed with nausea. His ears throbbed and the faces swarming around him were formless and distorted.

Maya appeared, gripped the young man's shoulders, and shook him. *You're going to be fine, we need to get you hooked in. Come on.*

A small gathering of huts met them deep in the decrepit forest. Maya pointed to one of the huts. The young man hesitated.

You have nowhere to go. You are in danger without Nadir. Let us help you.

The young man entered the hut. Three people sat facing away from one another bathed in the dim light of screens. Their skin was pallid beneath dense layers of paint, and their faces were fractured and macabre. On the screens they looked perfect. Pristine, gleaming and preternatural. Maya forced the young man to the ground in front of his own dim screen, half of which showed his face. He too looked perfect. Better, somehow.

The other half of his screen flashed brief clips of similar faces, sitting attentively and staring back at the young man. When a dancing woman flashed by, the young man's pupils dilated. The video of the woman's dance played until its end. The next video was a small dog, also dancing. The next was a hedgehog wearing a skirt. The young man thought this was absurd. The images started to flash by again until they stopped on a person wearing a mask and sitting motionless. Tiny numbers sprinted beneath the masked face—millions of interactions, untold numbers of eyes, entranced.

The masked person was unsettling. The young man grimaced. Tiny numbers flashed next to the young man's face over on the other half of the screen. As the numbers increased, watchers began to express their love for his reaction. Voices he could feel from mouths he could not see. Warmth surrounded the young man. His head nodded forward and his body became numb. But the voices became fewer and the nausea returned. When the next video flashed by he bellowed his disapproval of the circumstances.

When Maya returned to retrieve the young man, many cycles of the moon had passed. She carried the young man from the hut and rocked him to sleep.

The young man woke in a large room with solid walls and no windows. Enormous screens bathed the space in a weak blue hue.

The light spoke, *You have earned a place at a much larger table. One day, you will be like us. You escaped great sorrow and misery by coming to our land. We deserve your allegiance. You will disparage your forgotten home, that feeble prison of chastity. Say it.*

The young man responded weakly, *I will.*

With this grand destiny comes immense responsibility. You are a beacon of truth, a stark reminder of life outside The Interior. Entertain your master and you will drown in pleasure.

The blue light intensified and the young man cried aloud.

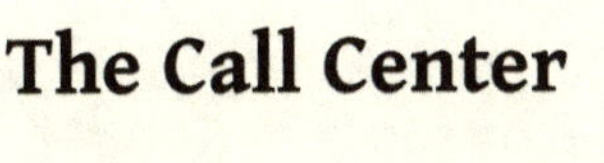# The Call Center

Today

Management called it The Pit in public, to inspire images of competition and victory, but in the honesty of closed door meetings they called it The Pen—a place for their animals.

Call center employees in The Pit were expected to have one thousand monetized conversations per week with strangers they were trained to hold hostage. Management insisted that life ebbed and flowed on the mercy of the sacred lists of leads—massive records of IT department victims that dwell in the shadowed nooks and crannies of *the market.*

Winston tapped his headset, "Yes, hello Jim, this is Winston O'Casey calling on behalf of...oh, yes, I understand. Yes sir, I'll make a note that you never want to hear from us again." Winston pretended to write down the complaint. "Yes, thank you, no need to get personal, sir. Have an excellent day." Winston put his head down on his desk. "The leads are utter garbage today."

The sun was abusive on the smoking patio— the last kicks of the Georgia summer. Winston lit a cigarette and took a seat on a concrete bench. A weak voice called from the edge of the patio.

"Winston." Stan limped from behind a tree.

"What happened to you?"

Stan coughed and held his side. "I should make this quick. They just fired me and did this to my face."

"Wait, you have blood all over you. Look at me, Stan."

"Listen to me, I'm fired, forever fired. They say that I sent some crazy email to the bosses. I'm being set up, Winston, and I think your new pal is behind it. I saw her in the hallway after all of this happened."

"You saw Mishra *here*, at the Call Center?"

"Right outside admin. Something's going on, I'd be careful if I were you. I have to leave now if I'm going to make it to..."

A massive boom shook their clothing and the concrete patio began to vibrate with a dull noise. Stan and Winston tried to run but nausea bent their knees and their stomachs emptied, splashing against the concrete. Beyond their heaving backs, the Pit had become a moaning din. A penetrating sound emanating from the walls and ceiling forced every employee to the ground, vomiting.

As his body convulsed, the light dimmed around the edges of Winston's vision.

The End

Winston

Six Weeks Ago

We made the right decision, but nothing had come easy or gone as planned. When we drove into Athens, Georgia, we had first and last month's rent, and little else.

I said yes to a call center job, jumping at the chance to have a steady paycheck. On the first sunny day of the summer, I put on a shirt and tie and drove beyond Athens' beltway to an anonymous forest. Beyond a cluster of Sugarberry elms, a squat, brick building emerged.

I was early, and apologized to the receptionist for it. She handed me a numbered badge with my name printed on it, and asked me to place my index finger on a digital tablet.

"No badge. No entrance. Walk down the hall and enter the second door on the left."

The second door opened into a wide, grey expanse surrounding a horseshoe of chairs and tables. An older man sat behind one of the computer tables and smiled when I walked in. I took a seat in front.

The rest of the training group began to slowly arrive.

—Eager: ten minutes early

—Competent: five minutes early

—Just-getting-by: 8am

—and the not-desperate-enough: 805-815am.

Our new manager was a full fifteen minutes late and made no mention of it. He slid into class and centered himself in front of two immense whiteboards.

"Hello everyone. Welcome to TelNet, I'm Josh. Does anyone have prior server administration, or server sales experience?"

Josh was very tan. His white argyle sweater paled against his charbroiled European skin. It was hard to take him seriously, especially when I noticed that his navy blue tie was speckled by tiny embroidered yachts.

The older gentleman who had arrived before me raised his hand.

"Yes, you sir." Josh pointed just over my head.

"I ran coordinating systems for UPS for twenty years, before they let me go."

"What is your name, and how did that touch on servers?"

"I'm Wayne. I chose the servers based on their compatibility with current systems and proposed changes."

"My, my, that's some rich experience, Wayne! Our friend Wayne here knows a little something about our target market. Pretty soon, Richie is going to come in and bring everyone up to speed on the exciting new products from HPBell that we're going to be forming relationships for. It's all very exciting. Bye for now, I'll maybe see you around."

Richie looked more like a bourbon and soda guy. He wore the Business Casual uniform, but carried himself with none of Josh's elite arrogance. Richie looked terrified of losing his job.

"Hey everybody. I'm Richie."

A young man called from the back, "Who was that other guy?"

"That was Josh. He likes to get a sense of new recruits. Have any of you worked in a call center before?" Four people sitting in a cluster, like family, raised their hands. "Did any of you work here?" No hands. "Good. Okay, welcome to TelNet. Today we start your training, take these and pass them around please." Richie handed a stack of papers to the closest person. "We're going to start by bringing everyone up to speed with what servers are, what they do, and why they interest our prospective leads."

An angry kid called from the corner, "Is this a sales job?"

"No. Thank you for asking, but if everyone will raise their hands before speaking, we'll have a smoother process. We don't do sales, we do introductions. When we make a successful connection, it gets sent to the real salespeople. We'll get to that. Does anyone have a background involving servers?"

The man didn't raise his hand a second time.

"Okay, that's fine, it's all in the handout getting passed around."

A pixelated logo, maybe a lion, sat at the bottom of the page as branding. The handout was high school curriculum quality, far below what I expected from a corporation.

A woman, closer to my age and wearing a shawl raised her hand. Richie gestured to her as papers were passed about.

"If we're not doing sales, what are we doing?"

"Well, on a basic level, we are contracted by companies that want to test desire for new products. Instead of having their sales team chase leads, they send their lists to us. We call these leads and talk to them. If they are willing to be contacted by the company's sales team, we send that lead back to the company as a win."

"How bad are the lists?" One of the call center-experienced students asked.

"That depends. Some of them are completely cold, but the vast majority are prior customers, so you end up talking to people who already like the company."

"Sounds like a cold call to me."

"Okay, does everyone have their handout? Good. Page three. *What is the Internet?*"

✕

I didn't know a whole lot about servers, but I could tell that some of the claims we were about to hurl at unsuspecting IT Directors were skewed. When we wrapped up the technical portion of the handout, Richie scanned the room again. "Let's take our break. We're going to dive into making calls next. Take the two doors at the back of the room through the call center floor. You'll see the break room, and beyond that is a patio if you'd like to step outside. Y'all have fifteen minutes starting now."

The conference room doors made a sucking sound as they were opened. A sea of voices in various stages of the same conversation flooded the conference room like a bright, unexpected light. I stepped out of the sound-proofed conference room into waves of ordered cubicle rows. The call center floor was massive; I guessed three hundred people sat at desks reading from scripts and ad libbing—I underestimated by more than half.

The training students formed a line, sensing they needed protection from the faces popping out of cubicles to sneer and glare at them. It was immediately clear that we were a threat, and the *pack* made it apparent that they would eat each of us alive if we disturbed the waters.

The break room was a vast cafeteria. Bench and round table seating consumed most of the room, a tiny kitchenette and a long bay of vending machines commanded the north and east walls. I watched a few people trickle out a side door beyond the seating.

The door tugged back at my hand, making the same sucking noise. The smoking patio was small, made smaller by a heavy circular bench and table. The bright cement space had no protective shade and the sun poured down in toxic waves.

The older man, Wayne from UPS, walked to my side and said from the corner of his mouth, "You seem like a nice kid. That's a real pack of degenerates in there, just watch yer'self."

"That seems like a pretty cheap shot against total strangers."

"Look, they're all criminals, and it's obvious that you aren't."

"You're right, I'm not a criminal."

"Then what are you doing here?"

"I needed a job."

"Every person in this call center's done something fucked up that landed them here. Why are *you* here..."

"Wayne!" Josh appeared, all gleaming incisors. "I thought we asked everyone if they'd worked here before."

"Yep," Wayne answered.

"Well, Wayne, it has come to our attention that you have, in fact, been in our employ previously."

"But that was for something different. I did my time at Merriwether..."

"That's enough, Wayne. Come with me please."

Wayne hesitated. Josh's expression never changed. The rest of the patio watched silently as Wayne relented and followed Josh back into the call center.

※

When we reported back, Caroline greeted us cheerily and took us to a cramped hall lined with tables and touch dial phones. We all took seats. Caroline walked around the room handing out login instructions for the call system.

"Everyone," Caroline waited until all eyes were on her. "Thank you. The handouts show you how to log in, and direct you to the project we will be working on. The system will dial the number for you when you click the contact. Remember, if someone is willing to discuss the product with you, ask for permission and record the conversation. The Quality Assurance Council will reject a lead that is not accompanied by a recorded conversation. Everyone understand?" She didn't wait for questions, "Good. Best of luck to you all. We expect you to make no fewer than 200 calls by the end of the day."

I did the math as I waited for my first victim to answer. They expected us to make about 30 calls per hour.

"Brandy & Jenkins Auto Body, Wendell here."

"Wendell, hey, thanks, this is Winston O'Casey. Are you the right person to talk to about servers for your..." Wendell hung up. I decided to mark Brandy & Jenkins *Undecided* for now. I clicked the next number.

"Yeah."

"Hello, this is Winston O'Casey calling on behalf of..."

"Which department?"

"IT Director if possible..." She was gone before I completed my sentence.

A man answered. "Yep."

"Hello, this is Winston O'Casey calling on behalf of HPBell."

"I can't approve sales, this is the help desk."

"No sales, HPB has a new line of servers they want to introduce your team to. Can I have an HPB sales rep. call you?"

"Sure."

I collected his contact information.

"And what's your title?"

"Customer Service Technician."

"Awesome, thank you. Have a good one."

"Yep."

I got one. I felt triumphant. I began to fill out the post-call data and stopped. I hadn't recorded the conversation. It had to be worth something that I had gotten over the wall so to speak. I completed the form and submitted the lead to the Quality Assurance Council. If nothing else, it made me look hungry.

Getting to the right person seemed like the first hurdle. Maybe if I didn't sound so guilty, already apologizing for the inconvenience. I dialed again.

"Winterspring Energy Services."

"Hello, is your IT Director in?"

"I'll need a name."

I stammered and searched the screen. "Andrew Livingston."

"He no longer works here."

"I'm sorry to hear that. May I speak to the current IT Director?"

"What is this regarding?"

"I'm calling on behalf of..."

"Direct all sales calls to 1-800-324..."

"Wait, I'm not a salesperson. I'm just reaching out to..."

"Please call 1-800-324-5657. Thank you for calling Winterspring Energy Services."

I re-dialed.

"I can see that you just called, sir."

I hung up.

I looked up the next company's name on the internet. I was able to locate a direct IT number. I dialed, proud of my redirection.

"IT."

"Is Daniel in?"

"Who is this?"

"Winston." I paused for too long. "I'm calling about the HPB servers."

"We got rid of HPB and their bullshit servers. I'm pretty sure I've asked a million times to be taken off this list."

"I'm sorry to hear that, Daniel..."
"Are we recording?"
"No, but we can be."
"Turn the machine on."
"This is Winston O'Casey speaking to..."
"Daniel Shepherd from Legacy Properties in South Tennessee. Go. Fuck. Yourself. Take me off this fucking list or so help me I'm going to drive down to your office and murder each one of you starting with Winston here. Do you understand? Dead people. All of them. Daniel Shepherd. Fuck you. Thanks and have a nice day."

An email alert popped across my screen.

Subject: You have to be kidding.

No recording, no lead. *Customer Service Technician* does not qualify as: "Director-level or higher, must be able to make commitments."

Try harder.
- QAC Division IV

The next twenty calls were grueling variations of rage, condescension, and the occasional *play along until it's time to commit* letdown. I planned my first micro-break for 11am but I didn't feel like I was going to make it. I clocked out of the system at 1030am and gathered my book and cigarettes. I began to resent that my time walking to the patio counted as my break; though it was an efficient way to prevent waste, the digital time clock removed any space for mercy.

The patio was empty and the sun had not yet cleared the meager stand of Poplars. I beat myself up for giving in so soon but vowed to take a short break and save a little time for the afternoon.

My alarm sounded before I'd finished half my cigarette. I hit snooze, like a lab rat. Every minute that slipped by was plagued by the thought: *there's another minute you can't breathe free later.* I crushed out the rest of my cigarette and rushed to my seat to clock in. I'd have fewer than ten minutes for my afternoon break.

✕

I made no headway by lunch, and I was not keeping up with my thirty calls per hour. I unwrapped my sandwich and tried to eat. When I couldn't finish the sandwich, I retreated to the smoking patio instead. Cliques huddled and individuals scrolled through their phones. I grabbed an empty spot; I was the frumpy goldfish in the center of the bowl. A second cigarette felt more important than eating and I timed it perfectly to end just as my last alarm sounded.

My call pace quickened, but I was still making no headway toward producing leads. I looked around the room wondering if anyone else was having as much trouble as I was. Everyone looked stressed, grey, and afraid. Our instructor sat silently behind a laptop, probably checking her social media accounts. I stretched, accidentally moaned audibly, and turned back to my console. I had wasted two minutes looking around.

At 230pm I convinced myself that I should take my final break. As I made my way to the patio I decided that I was looking at it all wrong. If I took a shorter lunch break I could section part of it into smaller breaks. I was already desperate to stave off madness, which was a bad sign. The pull to defy the clock and risk rebellion on the first day was strong, but we had bills to pay.

I completed my two-hundredth call at 502pm. I clocked out of my terminal and sat for a moment. My face felt numb. The traumatic day had robbed me of something and only silence could bring it back. My wife texted, *We're outside, can't wait to see you!* I trudged toward the exit.

"Wait!" The instructor was waving frantically to another door. "This is the exit."

"Oh, I came in through this door..."

She repeated blankly, "This is the exit."

My wife opened my car door. We kissed, and it felt like I was being rescued. I didn't cry, but I could have.

"How was your day?"

"It was strange. I'm going to keep looking, that's for sure. Making cold calls to people who erupt into rage is not something I'm super good at. Bizarre right?" I turned to our son in the backseat.

"Bizarre! Pops, what does bizarre mean?"

"Very, very strange." I leaned over to my wife, "Everything about it was fucking bizarre. I'll need to vent after the boy falls asleep."

"Oh no."

"I'll survive, my love. I've endured worse."

✕

On Friday, the receptionist sent me back to the grey conference room. I arrived later than I had the first day but I still beat most of the class. Wayne wasn't there, he hadn't been in the call room with us either. I felt bad that he'd been let go so soon, even though he seemed like a real asshole. Richie arrived fifteen minutes late, on cue it seemed, and announced that everyone in the room was moving on to the call center floor.

"You may notice that the group has gotten smaller, pat yourself on the back for sticking with it."

It felt more like we had submitted to something rather than overcome it.

"Today you'll get your cubicle in The Pit and be assigned a project."

"What's *the pit*?" someone called from the back.

"The call center floor. It's what we call it around here. I'll call out the names for team

Alpha, those teammates will follow me to their assigned desks. The rest will make up the other team. Sit tight for right now and I'll return to get you situated."

Alpha Team sounded like the team I wanted to be on. The *other* team didn't even get a name.

"Jenkins. Crenshaw. MacMillan. Stuart. Jones. Jimenez. Perkins. Lincoln. Washington. Espinoza. Merkovich. Okay, y'all follow me."

I wasn't on *Alpha Team* but at least I was employed. The rest of *other team* made eye contact, and a few of us said hello or started talking to old friends. No one else seemed to be concerned that they weren't called for *Alpha Team* so I tried to think about something else.

Richie returned. "Okay, is everyone ready?"

Other team followed Richie into The Pit. The hazing faces from the day prior had softened to smirks—a joke the rookies weren't in on. I was placed in a row with a cluster of veterans: a gentleman to my left, and two ladies to my right and aft. I said hello and smiled, it was a relief to be surrounded by friendly faces.

I started my computer and set up a notepad and pen.

A baritone voice called from behind me, "Hello there. I'm Maurice."

I turned and shook Maurice's hand. "I'm Winston, it's nice to meet you."

"Same. I'm a project lead, might not be your lead, but if you need any help you let me know."

"Hey Winston," Richie appeared behind Maurice, "are you all set up?"

"Yes sir, about to login."

"Good, your project will load when you sign in. Let's get going, the day's gettin' away from us. Hello, Maurice; I hope all is well."

"Everything is great Richie, thanks for asking. How's the wife?"

"Good. Okay back to work guys, 'preciate you."

I logged into the system and pulled up my lists. The more robust lists naturally attracted more eyes so I gambled and hit the smaller lists.

"Hey, Winston." Maurice was leaning around the cubicle wall. "Most of us are still human 'round here. Don't let them get to 'ya."

I smiled. "I won't Maurice, thanks." Maurice had a very subdued temperament, I wondered if he had become placid while making these abominable calls, or if his demeanor made him the perfect punching bag.

Maurice didn't smoke but he always went to the patio on breaks. He said that *there's something about getting out of the Pit that makes it possible to go back in.* His true passion was the blues, playing the blues, talking about the blues, and watching others play the blues. As much as he loved the blues, he loved his wife and son more.

"Hallelujah, it's good to be outside." Maurice stretched his arms toward the sky and smiled.

"It's brutal out here," I countered.

"We're outside Winston, ain't nothin' wrong with that."

"What are you up to this weekend?"

"Playing a little music on the outskirts of Atlanta. Next door to some of the best barbeque in the South."

"How do you do it, with the little ones at home?"

"They usually come along. My wife and kids stay in Atlanta and I go back and forth all the time. I got in a little trouble back in the day and I'm just wrapping up some unfinished business here."

"Then off to Atlanta?"

"Maybe." Maurice smiled. "Time's up."

My phone alarm sounded. And just like that, our brief reprieve was over.

✄

I also shared a cubicle wall with Kim Cookie. She had the gift; call after call she charmed, informed, and hit the record button. Her calls sometimes lasted for half an hour, but she had a close rate of 80%. She surrounded herself with personal items, fuzzy pens, photos of the grandkids, and spent all day, every day, wrapped in a large soft blanket.

Between calls, Kim would whisper across the aisle with Fatima. Fatima was reticent unless she was addressing Kim. The duo fiercely defended one another and Kim fawned over her pregnant friend in a motherly fashion. Their conversations were like a vast recorded history, each thread represented their true-life events. In the oral tradition of the ancient gods, they spoke their reality into being and gave life to the mundane and remarkable.

Before long, I began to understand Maurice's mantra. A brief refrain from the Pit was invigorating. The dull nausea produced by sitting in one's cubicle call after call, was briefly lifted once outside. One day, I took my lunch and wandered past the parking lot to a small forest of thin oaks. As I walked deeper into the trees, the crushing presence of the call lists and the desktop time clocks began to recede. My hopes returned as the sunlight became obscured.

In a clearing, I stumbled upon a series of graves. It was a family plot, the Daniel family. Between 1861 and 1864, they had lost twelve members, including three infants. The bigoted icons of humiliated slave masters adorned the adult male tombstones. I returned each day to eat my sandwich and smoke cigarettes in the solitude. Among the bones, my thoughts were clear and life seemed livable.

⋈

Kim Cookie raised her voice. "Are you sure now, honey?"

Fatima and Maurice stood to look over their cubicles so I followed along. Kim Cookie sat with her feet, clad in fuzzy night slippers, propped up on her desk. When she saw her audience gathered she raised her arms like a conductor.

"Now Terrence, you can't tell me that a 40% performance boost *and* a thirty-thousand dollar savings over five years is tough to go to the board with. Ain't no one askin' you to go to the board. Just hear out the HPB sales person, hell, you know how the economy is, you'll get a better deal out of them then you will through retail."

Kim signaled for silence.

"That's right. Yes. Yes, Terrence. Exactly. We have been recording, yes. I'll submit your name then. Okay. Always good to speak to you too, let the Wife know I said hey."

Kim ended the call. "Ooo, that's how you do it."

"Nice work, girl." Fatima reached across the aisle and gave her some love.

"Mm mm mm, no one better than Kim Cookie." Maurice smiled and held up his hands. "Say hey."

I held my hands up, "Hey."

"Thanks y'all. That lead ought to keep them off my back for a few weeks. Two more and I can get out of this project."

"You need to rub some of that off on me, girl. They're going to send me to Merriwether with my numbers."

"Fatima." Kim pulled her headset down. "Don't say that. Fuck, you know they listen."

"I know, I'm sorry, it just came out..."

"What's *Merriwether*?" I felt nauseated as I spoke.

"Another time, Winston. Just drop it." Maurice took his seat.

Five Weeks Ago

It was Friday, but it held no joy.

Maurice spoke softly to Winston. "You look pale. You alright?"

"Yeah. I think so."

"You gettin' sick?"

"No. It's weird, I'm just nauseated. A little bit; enough to matter."

"Only stops when you're smoking or when you go home, right?"

"Yeah, that's right."

"Don't let the job get you."

"*Get me*, how?"

"You see any happy people working here, Winston?"

"You seem happy."

"I have a family that loves me. Nothin' this place can do to take that away. Most people don't have that. Most people lost that along the way."

"Yeah. I have a family that loves me, so at least there's that."

"We're damned here, Winston. If you got something better to do with your days, I'd go do it."

Fatima returned to her desk without speaking.

Kim called across the aisle, "Girl, did you go over on your breaks again?"

"Yes. I could not bear to sit in this chair. I could not..."

"Don't test these people honey, they ain't your friends."

"They're sending me to Merriwether."

Kim stared, dumbfounded. "But, you've only been written up once. You don't deserve to be transferred. We can go to Kyle on Monday, he'll sort this out; your numbers are great."

"I'm leaving now. They told me to pack up my station and finish the shift in Merriwether."

"It's Friday, how can they..? This is discrimination. They can't treat you like this."

"Kim, please. I need this job, wherever it goes. I'm so close to finishing my parole, I cannot risk it now."

"People don't come back from Merriwether."

"I will, Kim. Don't worry yourself, god will protect me."

We all watched as Fatima cleared her desk of a few personal items. She was terrified, and we were all paralyzed: screaming inside to halt the injustice, but remaining collections of unwilling limbs and fearful minds.

"Maurice." Kim's voice was shaky. "This can't stand."

"It won't. I'm going to Richie."

"Wait, Maurice, I didn't mean you should..."

"It's the only thing I *can* do, and I have to do something."

It was hard to smile over the weekend. When I did, it felt weak. Not false, just shallow. It was nice to know our rent was covered, but being morose is a heavy price to pay. My wife began to wonder if it was worth it. Until we had another prospect, it had to be worth it. Maurice was on my mind. And Fatima, but Maurice's fate was still undecided. I was afraid for Monday, learning what came of Maurice talking to Richie, Fatima's empty desk, poor Kim, and as ever, the endless grind of the calls that undergird each crawling second of time.

⚔

Monday morning was a slow simmering panic attack.

"Hey, Maurice." I smiled, in hopes that it had a karmic effect.

"Hey, Winston. How was your weekend?"

"Fine, but I was worried. How did it go with Richie on Friday?"

"Don't worry yourself about that, Winston. It's out of our hands."

"And Fatima?"

"I should have minded my place. If I'm being honest."

"You're kind of scaring me, buddy."

"Don't be scared, be alert. Above all, stay alert."

"Stay alert? You have to be kidding."

"Don't raise your voice Winston, please."

"What is going to happen to Fatima? I need to know."

"You find out when it happens to you, not before."

"Winston." Richie appeared at the end of the aisle. "You have a few minutes?"

"Yeah, I mean yes, of course."

"Follow me."

Richie patted me on the shoulder like a brother.

Our section manager's office was tight, with a high, small window to the outside. It offered daylight but no view of the great turning world. A wall of glass faced the Pit, robbing the office of all privacy. Richie had no personal effects in the room.

"Have a seat, Winston. I wanted to check in with you, see how your first couple of weeks at TelNet have been."

"I haven't put a lead in yet, but I'm hopeful that by week's end..."

"Yes, that's fine Winston. I mean, how are you finding your coworkers?"

It felt like a set up.

"They're wonderful. Maurice is such a great guy, Kim is a ninja on the phone, and Fatima is an inspiration. Wherever she is."

Richie smiled, "Yes. Wherever. The thing that is puzzling to me is that *people like you* are not typically hired for the call floor."

"People like me?"

"You have more potential than your peers, Winston. I had the courtesy of reviewing your resume and I do wonder how you ended up here."

"We are new in town. I needed work, so I went to a temp agency. Here I am, nothing mysterious."

"Well, know that we expect great things from *people like you*. I'm sure if you get a few leads in I'll be able to make a case for putting a project under your lead. If that's alright."

"Sure, I guess that would be just fine."

✠

I leaned over Maurice's cubicle, "Why weren't you at break? I just had the weirdest conversation with Richie...are you okay?"

Maurice stared into the distance. His hands hung between his knees and his arms were limp.

"I got a call from my wife. She took our boy to the library." Maurice's chest heaved. "Someone followed him, our boy, into the bathroom and tried to trap him in a stall. They didn't catch the guy, but the police are there now and my son seems to be okay."

"Maurice, you have to go."

"Richie asked if I still needed to leave since the police had already arrived."

"Fuck that, Maurice. I can't believe you're listening to that asshole."

"The project is behind schedule, *my project.*"

"You're out of your mind, no job is worth...

"You're right. I mean, I'll go talk to Brian instead."

"Just leave, man."

"I can't..."

But he did. And he was not there on Tuesday. He wasn't there on Wednesday, Thursday, or Friday. I wanted to believe that he had walked away forever, but the framed pictures of his kids remained on his desk undisturbed.

Four Weeks Ago

The email felt like a friendly invitation, a brief pause in the calls. I entertained the possibility that I'd enjoy the re-training session. I was to report to a conference room on the other side of the building, far from the Pit. I overdressed that day—if I could be rescued from the Pit early, I'd give it a shot.

2PM finally arrived. I wandered down halls I had never seen, the numbering system for rooms felt random. We were made to form a line outside of the conference room until the meeting started. Our instructor arrived and we all filtered in and took seats around a large conference table.

"Hello everyone, I'm Dana. Make yourself comfortable, and grab one of the handouts."

The handout was another poorly photocopied mess. The front page featured a Zig Zigler quote.

"Welcome to the training session y'all. I want to start by walking through the process for our account communications and then open up the floor for your suggestions. Sound good?"

No one answered.

Dana guided us through a series of slides that mirrored our handouts. Self-helpy mumbo jumbo, cheerleading really. Maybe I was just getting disgruntled.

It was nice to discuss calls as an abstract concept, but it became clear that Dana had never made a call before. Her assumptions about the behavior of leads were way off base.

"You see, our numbers show that if you can get that pitch in within the first minute of the call, the chance of closing increases by..."

A woman called from the far side of the conference table, "What numbers?"

Dana was surprised by the interruption. "The numbers we collect as data here."

"Have you seen the numbers?"

"No, that's not really my..."

"You know what really works? Good leads. Not crashing in on people who hate HPB with a passion. Not cold-calling people who have moved on. We're wasting our client's time by calling recycled lists and TelNet is wasting my time by messing up my numbers."

The table murmured and Dana sensed she lost the room.

"We have to expect a high failure rate, otherwise our clients wouldn't pay us to review these lists."

"That's what we're saying," another woman joined, "if it's understood that we have a failure rate, what is the point of pushing us with unrealistic quotas?"

"They shouldn't be unrealistic..."

"They wouldn't be if the lists were decent. We're treated like we're failing, but it's the lists."

"I see. I am absorbing everything you are telling me. It's important for me to understand what would make your job more efficient and successful. We have to cut this short unfortunately, but I thank you for your candor."

The final slide had another bullshit quote about not giving up. The logo at the bottom of the screen read *Aslan Communications* and was next to a blurred shape, a lion.

"Thank you all for your time. I really wish we achieved more success. I don't feel like I *sold* you on the process. But that's ok, this was my first session so it can only get better with time."

I felt watched at my cubicle. I felt watched in the restroom. I felt watched in the parking lot, and I felt watched on the smoking patio. I was beginning to feel watched at home, but I was careful to not mention it to my wife.

The watching was part of the working conditions, but that day, beneath morose storm clouds, I could feel human eyes on me. I found my watcher as the end of my lunch approached.

She walked toward me without breaking our gaze.

"I am Mishra. It is a pleasure to meet you, Winston. May I sit down?"

"Sure. How do you know my name?"

"I am surprised that you are not in a Management program. How did you end up here?"

"I applied."

"Interesting. I didn't know that happened anymore."

"So, why are you here?"

"Good behavior. When a call program opened up I got shipped here to finish my sentence."

"Sentence?"

"Yes, sentence. Are you here because of the Merriwether facility?"

I wasn't sure. "No. I mean, I don't think so. Everyone seems pretty freaked out about this Merriwether place."

"It caught us off guard. This summer has been full of surprises."

"I'll be honest, Mishra, I'm a little confused."

"A fist fight is how I got here, Winston. I broke my racist teacher's nose. After that, I served a year in minimum security and got tapped for this work program."

"Seems like a harsh sentence."

"Cusseta is not what you'd call a progressive town. I was born in Georgia, but I do not look like I was. My father took a job with the criminal US military."

"Sounds like you disapprove of your dad's job."

"I do." Mishra offered no explanation. "Tensions were always high, and families like mine felt less and less welcome. How do you know Fatima?"

"I don't. Not really. She was close to Kim. You know Kim and Maurice, right?"

She smiled. "I do, yes. That is odd, Winston. Fatima attempted to send an email to you before she left on Friday. The company blocked the message and destroyed it."

"How do you know all of this?"

"I'd rather not say."

"Are you a hacker?"

"No."

"Cool, what kind of things do you get into?"

"Nothing crazy. You are sure, then; you do not know what Fatima was trying to tell you?"

"I'm sure, Mishra. I wish I could help."

"No, it is good that you are not involved. We are always being watched."

"By whom?"

"At present, by that man over there."

Mishra gestured to a balding man leaning against the call center wall. His face bore the lines of constant disappointment, and though he was studying Mishra and I, his disdain was apparent.

When the man started to walk toward us Mishra stood. "It was good to speak with you Winston, I do hope I have not caused you any trouble."

When the man reached our table, Mishra had already disappeared back into the call center. The strange man's suit was expensive and his hands were anxious. He loomed silently above me for several seconds before extending his hand.

"Hey. You can call me Stan. What were you guys talking about?"

Stan

Three Weeks Ago

I hate this town. I hate this state. I hate every fucking person I see, and every Confederate flag-draped porch. Bogart, Georgia represented my only shot at survival. I got real close, too close, to taking down the ex-mayor of New York City. I was sent to Rikers Island and the mayor delivered a goodbye message: three skinheads wielding sharpened toothbrushes. It's a miracle I survived. Getting as far away from New York City as possible was my only option, but Bogart was way *too far*, if you know what I mean.

The truth is, I'm a dead man no matter where I go. Truth is, I don't belong in a cubicle cold-calling with the rest of these animals. I'm smarter than they think, far more determined. Truth is, I belong to them. We've always belonged to them.

Management took their time before bringing me in. I'd been in the work program for eight months before I got a tap on the shoulder. My acumen and skillset didn't eclipse my felony. I reported to the conference room like a good little puppy.

Three young lawyer types walked in fifteen minutes late. The youngest, a man with wavy blond hair and a granite chin, spoke first.

"Mr. Stanislaus, thank you for meeting with us."

The eldest, a woman sharing the man's wavy blonde hair and impossible features. "We have a favor to ask."

The third crept into a corner and observed. He fell several evolutionary steps short of the Adonis and Venus he had arrived with.

"It's about time. You know I was a fucking lawyer in New York right? I could be running all kinds of..."

The young woman, "Mr. Stanislaus, may I call you Garrett?"

"Stan. I prefer Stan."

"Our recruiting practices tend to dictate the quality of personnel we have access to."

The young man agreed, "Yes, recent economic pressures have forced persons of, shall we say, *higher quality*, to end up in programs at TelNet."

The woman seated herself next to Stan and explained, "This opens doors to new variations of test procedures and processes. We are interested in tracking the performance of one of these candidates against our run-of-the-mill employee. Her name is Mishra Rana and she's on the 4th Quadrant HPBell project. Do you know her?"

"I don't speak to these ingrates. I am a member of the New York Bar. One in a long tradition of..."

"Ms. Rana strikes us as an odd member of the team. She came to us through the normal channels, but she has...*impressed* us."

The third man intoned slowly, "It's time to be part of the *'A' team* Garrett. If we don't keep the numbers up, we don't have a company. Do you understand?"

No, I didn't understand shit. "Sure. So I need to keep an eye on this loser, and then what?"

All three walked to the conference room door.

The woman spoke first, "We're counting on you, Garrett."

The young man spoke next, "Don't let us down."

And then the third, "It will be the last time you do."

They filed out in order, pretend-chatting like newscasters as the lights dim.

Working in the Pit meant sour guts and fluorescent blindness, the job was impossible without having a little fun. Without a little pushback against these aggressive swine, reasonable men would shriek in agony. The Catholic Church was, by far, my favorite to mess with...

"How many terabytes of kiddie porn do you store onsite at the Diocese, Father?"

"I beg your pardon?"

"What is your storage capacity onsite, in terabytes?"

"Well, we have a one petabyte SAN storage configuration..."

"One pedo-byte you said?"

"Um, yes, peta-byte. Did you just say...?"

"So you can store up to one pedo of files? I've heard you can actually store and protect thousands of pedos at the same time."

"Yes. I believe it is pronounced *peta*. P-E-T-A."

"Of course. Do you network your pedo of storage with pedos in other Diocese?"

"Look young man, I don't know if this is some kind of joke, but I don't appreciate..."

"No Father, this is no joke. Thousands of pedos all being protected by a single system is not just impressive, it's god-like."

click

Two Weeks Ago

Mishra was boring, kept her head down and just worked. She seemed to take more breaks than the average program worker, but according to Management, she's *special*. There was definitely no sense of command about her, she looked like a disgruntled teenager. What could possibly be so *special*?

It didn't matter. Management wanted eyes on her and I couldn't care less, I needed upward mobility.

I thought I was getting a break when Mishra started up a conversation with Winston. I was shocked to see her speak, much less to another employee. They seemed to hit it off right away. When Mishra pointed to me, I knew I had to fish or cut bait. She split as soon as I walked over, so I had a seat with Winston. He seemed alright for a white guy. Totally naive for a Los Angeles native, didn't even know the asshole's name that murdered Trayvon Martin.

Winston wouldn't tell me what he and Mishra were talking about, but I gained his trust. That's all that matters.

⋈

I waved a cigarette in the air as I passed Winston's cubicle. He nodded. I waited outside until he joined me.

"Good call, Stan. How's the day?"

"Fuck this place. Run by a bunch of Christian militants anyway."

"You know, I was meaning to ask you about that. I noticed that the teaching materials from our little training session reference a fictional lion."

"You don't know the half, brother."

"I'm not sure I *want* to know. This place isn't right."

"You know what I want to talk about? The fucking leads this week. It's like they're sabotaging us on purpose."

"I started working on the cleanup list so that I speak to fewer humans."

I was impressed. "Now that's thinking, Winston, good show."

"Problem is, most of the people are gone, as in dead, fired, or just plain gone. I started counting, nearly six out of every ten calls remind someone of a dead coworker and they burst into tears."

"You need to lighten up a little. These are moronic midwest IT employees that barely made it out of high school. When you call them, it's the first time they've wielded power over another human being in years, possibly ever. I've only gotten five leads past QA this week."

"Five? I thought you hated the leads."

"I'd have twenty by now if the leads were legit."

"I still have zero. What's your secret?"

"I pretend I'm handicapped. Like Stephen Hawking, or Corky from that TV show."

"Jesus Stan, that's fucked up."

"Why? They listen because they're no good assholes who pity kids in wheelchairs. If they weren't riddled with guilt, they'd politely decline and hang up. They deserve to be fucked over, they're the least among us, people who make *the list*."

"A list of assholes?"

"The master list. The kill list."

"You have a kill list?"

"Yep. Started it in third grade. It's a list of people to whom I owe a brutal death before I die."

"You are not a safe person, Stan. I need to get back inside."

Management was convinced that Mishra was special, but Winston was a dork. Unless Mishra was looking for a sidekick, I was barking up the wrong tree with Winston.

Today

As soon as my ass hit the seat, an email notification popped up on my screen:

—*Meeting in 30 minutes. Room 316.*

I replied—*Look, I'm feeling sick as hell. I need to go home.*

—*No. Room 316. 23 minutes.*

I was fucked.

I washed my face and hands in the Pit bathroom. I didn't know what was happening to me. If I had eleven faces, I'd have washed them all for the solace of control. I was powerless. It wasn't fair. I did the right things. I made the right people happy. But here I am, an indentured hand.

Room 316 was packed when I arrived. The only thing missing was a rope. The owner of TelNet remained seated and gestured to an empty chair across from him. I checked how many people I would have to get past to escape. Too many.

"Have a seat, Stan."

"Yes, sir. To what do I owe this robust gathering?"

"Come now, Garrett. Surely you..."

"No, you had it right, call me Stan."

"If you interrupt me again, Garrett, it will cost you your life."

I did not speak.

"Good. You understand. Here's the thing Garrett, thirty-four TelNet members of Management received abusive, vulgar, and frankly disappointing emails from your work account, gstan@telnet-dominion.org. The emails contained various threats of torture and death toward employees, their families, pets, and future families and pets. Including, but not limited to, extreme racist language and detailed depictions of rape and cannibalism."

"That's fucking hilarious. Why am I really here?"

The Owner stood and slapped me hard across the face.

"Why?" I got scared. "You didn't have to..."

He slapped me again, harder. "That's for what you said about my wife. We're all going to dispense a little justice on you today, Garrett. Pray we don't lose our heads."

Thirty four TelNet Management staff took turns slapping, punching, cutting, and spitting on me until I lost consciousness. When I woke, they were attempting to brand me with a crude cross formed by a bent paperclip. It burned like hell and I was able to kick a few of them away.

The Owner sat down while the other employees loomed over me. "You may have a head start, Garrett. It might be a small head start, but I'm feeling kind of generous today, so who knows? You should leave, though. As soon as possible."

I shuffled through the hall, bleeding. Then I saw Mishra talking to herself. We locked eyes and she bolted. Like an idiot, I shouted her name and gave chase. Mishra waved something in the air and I collapsed to the ground, writhing in pain. My guts felt like they were trying to escape my body. I watched her casually walk out of the building as I sobbed and pleaded. Then the nausea stopped. Just like that. Mishra was a ghost. Just gone.

I pulled myself upright and limped toward the exit.

Mishra

Eight Years Ago

I met Fatima at a Fort Benning mixer before either of us had heard of the School of the Americas. Our dads signed over their lives to the US government in return for shelter and the promise of petty labor. It was true that Nepal and Bangladesh were not safe, but rural Georgia put us in grave and dark danger.

The mixer was bizarre. My loud, commanding father was subdued. He bowed his head as he spoke to his military masters, played the jester and conversation maker. I did not recognize him. The crowd was segregated, it was clear that southern white men were the ones to impress and my father made haste attaching himself to whichever coven would open its wings.

Long chairs surrounding the host's pool provided quiet at a safe distance from the hob-knobbing. Across the vast azure surface, amidst the red, white, and sometimes blue decorations, Fatima's eyes stopped on mine. I waved hello and she smiled. We were the same age, just children. We went on to attend the same schools in Clarkston until her father made a hurried exit from Georgia and public life—well, public life as we knew it.

I fantasized for many years that my father would also be *called back* and Fatima and I would be reunited. But my best friend's father had not been *called back*; he had fled for his life. My father let it slip during an argument with my mother over returning to Nepal. She begged him to reconsider, to *remember who we were.* He struck her and she cowered while he screamed about loyalty and blood. I like to think my mother had no choice, but she left me with him and escaped. Some people said back home, most assured my father that she was not *that stupid.*

I kept my head down and paid attention to my studies and reputation. As long as those two things remained above reproach, my father was uninspired to meddle in my affairs. Through my high school years he was a ghost, appearing and staying for days, sometimes months, but inevitably returning to a far off assignment. I was granted the space and the resources to express my latchkey angst by penetrating and disrupting corporate data networks. I evolved; I had no control over my chaotic life, but I had mastered weapons that destroyed control systems with fire.

✂

On my nineteenth birthday I received a message that put me on my present course.

Sister-
It is Fatima. Go today, and bring your laptop:
143 Alabama St SW ATL
3rd floor north wall
The only letter for you and me.

My father was out of the country so it was simple to steal his car keys. I removed the tracking device from the engine compartment and placed it on a shelf. I was in Atlanta by nightfall, parked the car in Frog Hollow, and took the MARTA train to Five Points.

The Five Points station was crawling with Sheriff's deputies in body armor. Red, white, and blue sirens created a disorienting cloud of light. I rushed across Forsyth Street to 148 Alabama, the long abandoned Atlanta Constitution building. The farside parking structure provided shelter from the police occupation across the street. The third floor was cluttered with debris, and the walls were clogged with graffiti. I scanned for *The only letter for you and me.* I was missing something. A large, unspoiled mural of an immense all-seeing eye covered the back corner of the structure. How clever, Fatima.

A USB stick had been hidden in the center of the eye's black pupil. The connection side protruded from a slot in the brick wall. I connected my laptop to the device and transferred the files to my computer. The first file commanded me to *Find the large rock at the base of the mural. Use it to smash this USB stick to pieces. These files cannot find their way into the authorities' hands.*

I found a small boulder on the ground. Though I struggled to lift it above my head, I brought it down hard on the plastic device.

⚔

That night I learned that Fatima had been taken prisoner. Her father was accused of conspiring to sell intelligence to foreign powers. As Fatima planned her high school graduation party, the adult men in her family began to disappear. Women and children were plucked one by one and sent to live in cramped detainment camps. In a stolen moment, her family had vanished. Several years into her incarceration, Fatima was selected for a government program. She had no illusions and expected it to be brutal, but the program involved living off-site, getting a chance to pretend everything was normal.

The program was far from normal. The campaign, as she described it, was a prolonged experiment to test the boundaries of human endurance. The Call Center was a constantly churning machine with thousands of rules to be broken and impossible goals to meet. Punishment was heavy-handed, and often, people simply disappeared. Reassigned to a facility named Merriwether, never to return.

I need your help, Mishra. I'm not sure how they are controlling us, but I know it is orchestrated by the IT department. I wouldn't involve you, but I cannot do this alone. I will send further instructions. If you choose to run away from this, I will understand. I wish you peace.

✘

School was stifling. Fatima had left years ago. Only rumors existed around her whereabouts. Speculation by ignorant racists and bootlickers.

"Mishra. Are you paying attention?"

The chemistry teacher was staring at me, and soon the entire class joined him.

"This is important, Mishra. Even where you come from. Let's move on. If we introduce more peroxide to the hydrochloric acid solution, it will begin to dissolve the flesh of the..."

I interrupted him. "Do you actually know where I come from?"

My teacher smirked. "Where you come from doesn't matter. You don't matter. But the rest of these kids do, so keep your mouth shut..."

"Is that what happened to Fatima? She didn't keep her mouth shut?"

My teacher did his best to puff his chest and look menacing, but he would not approach my desk. "I know our military thinks having pet foreigners running around is clever, but where I come from, you don't invite cockroaches in, you stomp them."

I stood and walked toward the teacher's desk.

"Mishra. Take your seat or so help me, I'll..."

I slapped the final words out of his mouth, drawing blood.

My teacher's grin bore a centuries-old hatred, the knowledge that no matter what gruesome plan he had for me, the color of my skin gave him the right to execute it. "That was a big mistake."

I closed my fist and struck him again. Before he could recover I struck him again. When he stumbled, I buried my boot in his stomach. I pummeled him until students pulled me away. Four boys avenged their mentor and dealt powerful blows to my face and sides, but nothing could penetrate my calm.

They skipped expelling me and I was immediately placed in a detainment camp near the Florida border. I survived three hundred eighty-nine days amid barbed wire and repeated solitary confinement before I was selected for the TelNet program.

Three Weeks Ago

I was relieved that I had spoken to Winston. He was the only TelNet employee without a criminal record, and when it all hit the internet, he'd be the only credible source white America would listen to. I endured much to come to this place of suffering. I failed Fatima, but I will not fail again.

Management left a note on my desk, *Conference room 316 3PM, please bring your files.* Conference room 316 was deep in the C-suite wing of the facility. The lights above the wide oak table were blinding and the room was frigid. *Same old bullshit tricks.* The walls were barren save for an inspirational verse, *Cast all your anxiety on him because He cares for you.* I took a central chair at the table and folded my hands in front of me.

On cue, a parade of executive hubris filed into the room. VP of Finance, VP of Human Resources, VP of Operations, and VP of IT; it was a cloud of blonde, styled hair, casual aryan eyes, and muddled mouths, tense with privilege. The replicas took seats and sat down in congress.

"Let me begin by saying that we are very disappointed in your behavior, Mishra." — Operations.

"Indeed. Some alarming concerns have been raised regarding your activities." —Human Resources.

"Moreover, we have proof." —IT.

Finance remained silent.

"Do you know what we are talking about, Mishra? It would be a good time to be frank with us. It can only help." —Human Resources.

"Yes, a little something from you may go a long way, Mishra." —Operations.

I answered as calmly as I could muster, "You'll have to be more specific. My behavior is often viewed as offensive."

"You've been gaming the timecard system." — IT.

"Jesus Christ, Larry." —Operations.

"Sorry." —IT.

—Operations, "We know that you've been remaining clocked in regardless of long absences from your station. You are on a fastrack back to a state prison cell."

But no one brought the cops so this is about something else...

—Human Resources, "Mishra, we believe in *redemption* here. Were it not for our faith in the one true god, we could not muster the pity to maintain this facility and continue its important work. By god's grace, we have a proposal. If you are willing to consider this proposal we can make certain promises. Do you understand?"

"Yes."

Finance finally spoke, "We are besieged by scum like you: illegals, subversives, and perverts trying to undo god's work. What we need is a poisoned mind like yours patching up our weak points, working closely with Larry to shore up our defenses. You committed a serious crime Mishra, that's why you're here, and you know the consequences of our arrangement not *working out*. We are prepared to deport you to a very remote, very concealed, Federal facility."

"Can you take this opportunity to stand in god's glory, Mishra?" —Human Resources.

"Yes, god willing."

"That's good, Mishra. Please, go with Larry." —Human Resources.

Larry was not pleased. I knew more about TelNet's system than he did, that much was clear. He could never comfortably *know* what I was doing.

My new desk in the bowels of the server room featured a chair fitted with restraints.

"Have a seat, Mishra." Larry slowly strapped my legs to the chair. "If you have to take a piss, message me. Hopefully, I'm not too busy." Larry pulled the final strap a bit harder than necessary. "If you fuck up, even a little, you're as good as deported, got it?"

"Yes, Larry. I mean, yes, sir."

"That's right."

✕

Late that afternoon I bounced a set of stolen credentials against the TelNet personnel files. They kept a tight ship there, but it allowed me to take a bridge into *Operations, Projects,* and then *Research*. I was right, Fatima's pregnancy was being monitored, but there was no record of her transfer to Merriwether. She just disappeared. They were also looking at Winston. Why hadn't they sent Winston away? The details were locked behind a firewall offsite at Merriwether. Any attempt I made to breach it would be detected easily. I would need to hack their system in 3D, plug in directly and cross my fingers.

TelNet seemed to be like most companies, spending more on digital security than physical security. It meant we had to change up our tactics. If it's easier for me to get a USB stick into a server room than it is to create a digital tunnel, so be it.

Larry called from the hallway, "Mishra, it's time to get out of here." The jangle of my jailer's keys preceded him.

I covered my tracks and shut my computer down.

"Hey Larry, don't forget to let me out. Larry. Larry?"

He didn't forget, and I spent the first few nights strapped to my chair.

Two Weeks Ago

Merriwether was in Carnesville, GA: population 599. The forty minute drive was nerve-racking. Endless curving two-lane roads consumed by trees and an ominous darkness. All it took was one curious Sheriff's deputy and I could be on the receiving end of a hate crime.

I left State Route 106 and turned in front of the Carnesville City Hall. Like so many other backwoods southern towns, it was tarnished by a cheap statue commemorating the defeated Confederacy. The tiny town also had a state prison crawling with cops. The odds were bad for me if I got caught.

I shut off my headlights and pulled into a small public park with a few cars in its lot. I ran into the treeline to approach Merriwether on foot. The summer foliage was dense, but keeping my distance from the main facility was my only hope at stealth. The forest receded at the rim of a massive sewage processing pit, bound by a surface of bright green algae.

Beyond a nine-foot fence was Merriwether; it was nothing more than an elementary school. Children's swing sets, playgrounds, and a low brick modular building were flanked by an immense prefabricated warehouse. The compound was still, and the lights were out.

The loading dock was dark and I made it to a side door quickly. The door was a simple deadbolt, they didn't seem to be afraid of someone finding out what was inside. Come to think of it, there had been no motion sensor lights either.

I popped the lock and slowly pulled the door open. It was very cold inside. The dense summer heat evaporated as I crossed the threshold into the Merriwether facility. The hallways were silent, vacated. The kitchen was bereft of pots, pans, and signs of food. The back walls and hallways were crushed with dozens of locked freezers lining the walls, stacked, at times, five tall. Each freezer had a series of numbers stenciled on its long side.

The facility was composed of holding cells with chains and restraints, bizarre machinery, and cramped surgical rooms. The last hallway terminated with a set of offices. I found the purpose of the numbering system in a thick manual sitting open on a cheap plastic desk.

The names of the abducted and exiled were cataloged and organized into campaigns, to test the veracity of their theories. I found Fatima's name and threw the manual to the ground. The thick book created an echo down the long halls and I froze.

The office's lone desktop PC used PASSWORD as a password, and had much deeper access than the call center IT group. I plugged in a drive to scrape everything I could access and rested on my heels to wait.

A voice in the distance startled me. It was very faint, but definitely a human voice. I encouraged the download to fucking hurry. When the file transfer ended, I unplugged the USB and shut down the computer. The voice got louder toward the back of the building and the closer I dared to get, the more it seemed like the voice was coming from the warehouse outside. After listening intently I realized it was repeating the same short block of words. It was a recording.

The warehouse was a brightly lit surgical amphitheater. In the center of the room a long adjustable table, sanitized by chemicals, gleamed under the overhead lights. A slow incantation droned over loudspeakers: *Slaves, be subject to your masters with all reverence, not only to those who are good and equitable but also to those who are perverse."*

Standing bleachers encircling the surgical table rose to the thirty-foot high ceilings. Cameras lined the amphitheater to memorialize each criminal act. Their vanity would once again speed their demise.

✗

Hiding in a south Atlanta diner, I pulled up a schedule from the USB, but I wish I hadn't. There were so many names. Tens of thousands of human beings processed through dozens of facilities. A vast net culling the population in order to play out their sick fantasies. They kept meticulous records of every torture, every unnecessary medical procedure, and each casualty.

Fatima was their latest victim. They anesthetized her, induced labor, and pulled her baby from her womb. The viability test failed and the little one died soon after entering the world. Fatima became *...inconsolable, and brutally assaulted several members of the scientific staff.* Rather than proceed with the hysterectomy, they murdered her with a lethal injection of ketamine...today. She died today.

Fatima emailed Winston to lead me to Merriwether and I was too late. I wanted to burn Merriwether to the ground, but I had to wait.

⋈

"Sanjay, it's me."

"I know."

"I had to make sure this would be a completely private conversation."

"I understand. Are you alright?"

"Yes and no. No, because I am in danger. But yes, because I have a plan and it will prevail."

"How can I help?

"I need to dump a data set into a nice little package and send it to various TBD locations for safe-keeping. I will have the keys to the castle."

"Since you're calling me, you must need it to come from outside."

"Way outside."

"This will only give you a few days' jump."

"That's all I have. I'll send the necessary documentation to Bishkek. I am sorry that you will have to go into the city, but I cannot risk this information traveling digitally."

"I understand. So you'll leave the door unlocked, I'll grab everything that's not nailed down, and run."

"Grab everything nailed down as well. The process I'm putting in place is going to nuke the homebase, so we need all of it."

"Are you sure you're okay?"

"Yes and no, remember? If they catch me and put on a show trial, no one will notice. If I can get a head start, people will have time to learn what's going on here."

"What is going on there?"

"They'll be on my doorstep that morning, so I'll send the execution date and leave the details in the usual places. Once I escape, it may be some time before I can raise my head again. I thank you for this favor, my friend."

"Of course, what are stateless hermits for?"

Today

When I arrived at the Call Center a low grey mist obscured the entrances and windows. In past times I would have taken this as an ominous sign to abort. The Management-side halls were empty but the roar of the Pit remained. I was always the first in, which gave me time to prepare before the bosses arrived.

But today, my boss was tapping away at his laptop with a worried look on his face.

"Everything okay, Larry?"

"No."

Larry's brow was wet with perspiration.

"Someone hacked Merriwether last week."

"Oh shit."

"Yeah. And they used an old set of credentials that *should* have been turned off."

"Oh man, are there any other credentials we need to shut down, just in case?"

"Just yours." Larry turned his laptop. Video footage of my masked, hooded head walking throughout the facility played silently. "They might actually kill you for this. Did you think about that? Anyway, I'm definitely getting promoted for installing those hidden cameras..."

Without thinking, I grabbed the server room fire extinguisher and bounced it off Larry's forehead. He was still breathing, so I didn't have much time. I strapped Larry to my chair and duct taped his mouth closed. Larry and I waited and watched the security monitors while morning at TelNet began.

The Management parking lot started to fill up and Larry began to stir. I popped him in the head again so that he'd sleep through the reckoning. "You're welcome." I opened Sanjay's digital backdoor and confirmed she was connected. Once the Call Center's files were secure and I cranked up the sound torture, I'd only have a few seconds to flee.

As I locked the server room door Winston's shadow spotted me. I had to use the sound torture against him, but I couldn't risk being stopped. I couldn't risk failing again.

A Carnesville Horror

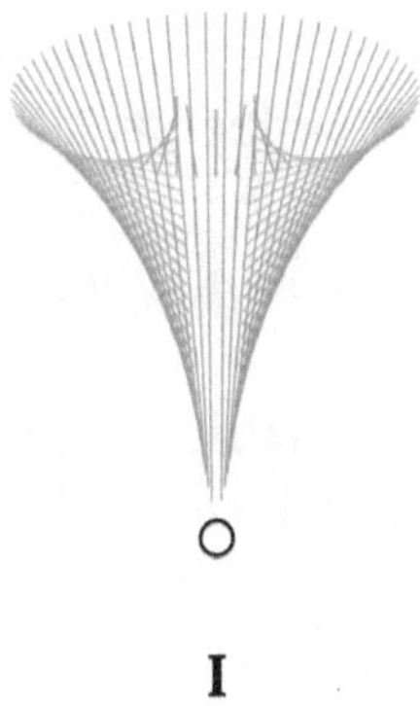

I

As for these events,
You may have reality now,
But nothing is eternal.

The hot humid nights were torture. The lease was up, the money had run out, and eventually Ian would need to ask someone for a loan—the great American admission of failure. He found a reluctant host, a temporary sofa to sleep on, but began to sink into a deep well of fear. With each passing day the top of his prison receded farther and farther away.

Ian received a text late in the evening.
　　—Are you still looking for work?
　　Ian answered quickly. —I am.
　　—Can you meet up near campus sometime next week?

—Of course, let me know where and when. For the record, I'm available this week as well.

—Excellent. Let's meet at Little Italy, 3p, next Thursday.

—See you there! Thank you, Søren.

Ian drove into Athens, Georgia and parked downtown to enjoy a brief walk. Being in Athens, on those quaint sidewalks so close to his old office, summoned feelings of vengeance. Ian's ex-boss fired him on a Monday for talking back on a Thursday. The termination was immediate and Ian was left without income or health benefits while the pandemic still raged.

Søren was sitting across from a stranger at a table near the restaurant's front window. The men stood as Ian entered.

"Hey man, it's good to see you." Ian shook Søren's hand and hugged him.

"Ian, this is Dr. Basil. He is a professor at UGA and a close colleague."

"It's good to meet you. Dr. Thoiaker speaks very highly of you."

"Thank you, doctor. It's a pleasure to meet you."

"So, Micah, would you like to brief Ian on the assignment?"

"Yes, of course." Dr. Basil pulled a small orange USB drive from his leather satchel. "I have a substantial amount of data that I need reviewed, organized, and eventually presented for a layperson's consumption. In short, I need to dump research on you and have you transform it into actionable work in a short amount of time."

"Sounds like a good time to me. What will I be reading about?"

"An apocalyptic cult in rural Georgia."

"Nice. Did they off themselves?"

Dr. Basil gave Søren a disappointed look. "No. This cult is more of an oddity. The problem is that they've gone underground. Far enough underground that we'd like to know why."

"Okay. What flavor of ghost story do these folks believe in?"

"This is an oversimplification, but in essence, this group believes that an entire pantheon of gods exist and make up 'capital R, Reality.' The true reality that is beyond human comprehension, et cetera. These gods are purely spiritual and paired as male and female emanations from the one true god—itself a female and male pairing.

"One of the gods birthed a child, without the assistance of its counterpart, and outside of the one true god's permission—a virgin birth, if you will. The child was born a monster: imbued with its mother's magic, but malformed, ignorant, and flawed. Depending on which version of the story you read, this child either flees or is banished to a place where it is separated from the rest of the gods. In an act of heretical arrogance, the child emanated its own demi-gods and created our universe.

"Where true Reality is spiritual and eternal, this child god's reality is material, and thereby doomed to death. The child god deceives humanity in various forms throughout our history, boasting that it is the one true god and that there is none above it."

Ian smirked. "Sounds familiar. You mentioned the apocalypse, did they go underground after the end times never came?"

"Excellent, now you're asking the right questions." Dr. Basil smiled. "There is no specific prophecy regarding when, only how and why. In their view, the serpent from the creation story is a hero. Knowledge of good and evil was the first step toward liberation from the flawed god. A gift to humanity, possibly from the child god's mother. Their *apocalypse* is a final battle between the child god and the one true god. But first, the child god must be released from its prison. Instead of preventing the monster's release, this group sought to hurry things up. They published extensive pamphlets and interpretations of traditional scripture for decades, then suddenly stopped. We have not found evidence for their exact whereabouts. Yet."

"Is that where I come in?"

Dr. Basil straightened his back, "I need someone to engage with this body of material, really absorb and understand the data. How do you feel about that?"

"Excellent. Right up my alley." William folded his napkin in half. "You already seem to know this group pretty well."

"I know their mythology very well, religion is my true passion. I felt called to astronomy and the wider cosmos late in my career. Perhaps to make this very moment possible." Dr. Basil was satisfied. "I'll draw up an agreement for Mr. Mhealladh. I want to get to work as soon as possible."

"Work will begin today, professor. Thank you for this opportunity. Søren, I'm going to head out, I have a long drive ahead."

Søren looked confused, "I thought you lived a few blocks from downtown."

"I used to. Matt fired me. I've been crashing at a friend's place in Atlanta."

"That's no good, Ian. You are welcome to come stay..."

Dr. Basil interrupted. "I have a friend whose home remodel has been put on indefinite pause. If you don't mind keeping the place tidy, they'd be pleased to collect rent."

"That's very generous of you, Dr. Basil. I'm a tidy person, and I don't mind looking after the place. I can only afford what this contract will allow, so if your friend doesn't mind cutting me a break..."

"Say no more, Ian. Here's the address. Loida will be overjoyed; the place is sitting empty while construction is halted."

"I am definitely in your debt, Doctor."

"You're doing me a great service, do not mention it."

※

On the last normal Sunday of his life, Ian drove out to the city of Carnesville to see a large white house on a heavily-wooded lot. Carnesville was out there, like thirty miles to a proper grocery store, out there. The virus was still rampaging through the countryside, and Ian was happy to be as far from Atlanta as possible.

Carnesville, population 599, had all the trappings of "rural Georgia," including a cheap confederate monument on the city hall lawn, and nothing but cows, forests, and fields as far as the eye could see. If not for its proximity to Interstate 85, Carnesville would have melted into the greater redneck apocalypse, unseen by foreign eyes.

The house was on a small side road and faced the backside of a gas station on Georgia State Route 106. Behind the freshly-painted, two-story house lay an acre of cleared yard and a massive forest beyond. The white house was tall and stark against the lush green backdrop, the final house on Athens Street. It was built for a racist judge turned politician in the late 1800s, and was still revered for being a part of the town's *heritage.* The only neighbor was a large Victorian house surrounded by massive Water Oaks and a lone Magnolia tree with a tire swing. A wide side yard to the east separated the homes, and to the west, the Carnesville house held an acre of dense forest that wound along Route 106 to Stephen's Creek. The owner showed Ian through the house; it was way too big, a home fit for raising a family. The wide open backyard, enclosed by a wall of trees in the final throes of summer, was a grand emerald refuge from the world gone mad.

As Ian unpacked his small car, wide black wings painted shadows on the rising green grass. Six massive buzzards swept through the yard and gathered on the tin roof of an abandoned metal storehouse across the street. The beasts' claws clicked against the ancient metal roof and echoed down the lonely end of the street.

No one would notice if the forest swallowed him whole. Separated—confined by distance and time—Carnesville would now be his reality, a distant, isolated island in an emerald sea—adrift beyond the walls of civilization.

Once everything was moved in, Ian removed the American Flag from the front porch. He despised flag-waving, and during such divisive times, it felt even more sinister. Carnesville, Georgia was far away from everyone Ian knew, far from all of his friends ignoring the pandemic, far enough away for his feelings of betrayal to cool. Surrounded by the trees and silence, Ian settled into the Carnesville house to lick his wounds.

Winter still gripped Seth's cramped college town and the surrounding forests remained sparse and skeletal beyond the vernal equinox. The afternoon was no different than thousands of afternoons she had spent on campus. Most of the students were already away on break, and Seth planned to wrap up the semester's grading so she could flee as well.

Budget cuts at the university forced tenured staff like Seth to lend a hand wherever possible. Even if that meant reviewing pre-grad papers using obscure religious cults as supporting evidence.

It appears that as the surviving dogma of the modern church was being formed, groups like the focus of this paper were nearly exterminated:

"We are a hunted and tormented people. By the very nature of our knowledge, we are targeted by the heretical sects. Blinded and coerced as they are by their tribal god, they have now poisoned the mind of an Emperor."

They considered evil the result of greed, which is most barbarous when guided and cultivated.[1] It is not our nature, it is our aberration—fed and fertilized by blood and conflict. We are not genocidal by nature, but when we get together and plan for the future, all bets are off.

Seth yawned; Dr. Thoiaker had some odd students. Seth wished for a distraction and her phone buzzed on the wide lecture hall desk.

—Hey, it's Ashima.

—I know. You're texting me from your phone.

—I'm not good at starting text conversations *crazy face emoji*

---

[1] *Our Greatest Betrayal* (Q. Tedros 1st edition 1989, p. 21): "The many plagues of this century have weakened reason and skepticism. Fear rules the day and violence is the chosen language and expression of this Fear. Calling the ancient storm god by its true name is now blasphemy, punishable by torture unto death. The cult of the end times now courts eternal dominance, squaring the contradiction and wresting unchallenged power by force."

—Straight to the point. No emojis. Ever. I have a few more papers to grade, then I'm free to leave town. I won't stand for frivolous distractions.

—Start thinking about what you would name your first major discovery. Our first major discovery.

—Matilda, after my mother.

—Keep thinking about it while you analyze the data I just sent over.

—I don't have time for this.

—Trust me, you do. I have a date this evening, so don't expect me to answer any late night calls *eyes emoji*

—Don't worry, I won't be calling. Who is she? Anyone I know?

—None of your business.

—Ah, so I do know her.

—Prefers him.

—Then tell him to treat you right or half of north Georgia will be after his ass.

—Everyone knows I'm the most protected girl in the program.

—Good, it's not safe there.

—And it's safe in Georgia?

—No, but in Arizona you're two-thousand miles away.

Seth closed the department's laptop and rubbed her temples slowly. The semester was complete, she could disengage soon. Ashima's frantic push would have to wait until Seth was in another state of mind, preferably with an adult beverage in hand.

"Hey," a man approached from the top of the seating gallery. "Professor Set, right? Are you still using this room, or can we close it off for cleaning? The staff wants to know."

"Seth. I prefer Seth. Yes, I am done, just daydreaming about leaving this place for a while."

"Don't wait, just leave."

Carnesville lacked sidewalks, which turned Ian's casual strolls into arduous hikes. Long, winding, Summer lanes gave way to pastures, livestock and the bent lines of sunset over distant forests. Beyond these agrarian estates lay a nest of tangled byways along river beds and sewage paths. Houses in these tucked pockets bore the neglect of forgotten people. No one had lifted a finger to take care of this part of the population, the understanding was that they were to be erased. Slowly, if necessary.

Three solid knocks broke Saturday morning silence and Ian froze.

"Who the fuck is that?"

An immense man filled the front door window, politely looking to the side rather than peer into the house. Ian pulled a mask from his back pocket and opened the front door.

The man smiled broadly. "Sorry to bother y'all, but I wanted to say hello and welcome. I'm Christian." He extended a massive paw to shake Ian's hand.

"Hello, I'm Ian."

"It's good to meet you. My wife Bernette and I have been keeping an eye on your property for quite a while." The neighbor started walking the length of the front porch.

"Oh, ok. I'm just renting, but thank you. Nice and settled in now."

"Good, good. They did a lot of work on this place." Christian looked around like a foreman.

Ian could tell Christian meant to visit, so he walked onto the porch and shut the door behind him. "They left a bunch of materials out in the forest too." Ian pointed. "There are two huge piles of dirt and bricks, looks like a couple of fireplaces came down."

"Yep. Shame they had to take down the fireplaces. They had to replace the foundation too. Jacked the whole house up a few feet at one point, it was somethin'. They had to be real careful, disturbing the original crawlspace is forbidden. If it wasn't for the lockdowns, I think they'd probably have worked on it for a couple more years. Tough market these days, though."

Christian was not wearing a mask, but he didn't leer at Ian like the people at the gas station did. "Well, I'm glad they were willing to take renters, it worked out nicely for me." Ian forgot that no one could see him smile.

Christian sized Ian up. "It was a sudden change in our mission, and not much changes around here. That's how the old-timers like it. You could say they're a little stuck in the past."

"What about the rest of us?"

"The rest of us don't own all of the land in Franklin County, so we're just along for the ride."

"I see."

"In the 60s this place was supposed to be a new hub between Atlanta and Lake Hartwell. When I-85 was built we had a big population explosion and then it just stopped."

"Stopped?"

"The old land owners pumped the brakes. Now, most people leave Carnesville as soon as they graduate from high school—sooner if they're lucky. Most never come back..."

"So the town is dying."

"Looks that way. Maybe we'll outlast the old guard. We'll have to see. Well, I won't keep 'ya. Just wanted to say hello. If you need anything, don't hesitate to holler at us. Hey, we're church-going folks, non-denominational you could say, so if you're looking for a church home..."

Ian shook his hand again, "Thank you, Christian, I'm all good in that regard."

"Where do you attend, if you don't mind me asking?"

"I don't. Attend, that is."

Christian flushed red. "Oh. Well, that's your choice I suppose. I didn't expect Loida to rent outside of the flock."

"I have a feeling I'll be your favorite neighbor of all time. It was good to meet you."

Christian ambled back to his side of the property line. He was several inches taller than Ian and outweighed him by at least two-hundred pounds. There's no way Christian could catch up to someone like Ian, but if he got his huge paws around his neck, it would be game over.

Ashima's date was a no-show. She was surprised, he had been adamant about the time and location. The no-show was doing her a favor, best to see a red flag early and avoid the drama. Men in white dress shirts and khaki slacks marched toward the quiet cafe and Ashima craned her neck to watch them pass. It was the same flavor of bigoted ruffians she'd seen all over Flagstaff. To these men, "Pride" was only a dirty word if it involved rainbows and puppy play.

They were terrified that someone was conspiring to "replace" them, but the all-powerful "someone" that plagued their feeble minds changed frequently. Soft as a whim, their masters spoke a new enemy into existence and their hatred was redirected.

The no-show called.

"Hey, sorry I'm late, I'll be there soon. Got stuck but still coming!"

"No worries, but don't bother. I'm getting ready to head out. I have to be at the observatory pretty early."

"WAIT," he raised his voice. "Please don't leave. I'm sorry, it wasn't my fault..."

"What is your deal? Nothing about this conversation makes me comfortable with seeing you."

"It's important. You just have to wait."

Ashima ended the call and blocked the no-show date.

As she gathered her jacket and books, Ashima could feel the marching men's eyes on her. She was not a stranger; her presence gave them suicidal purpose. As she reached to open the cafe door, a blunt object struck her head and she collapsed. The cafe's security camera captured a man breaking rank from the march to strike Ashima, knocking her to the ground and kicking her with all of his might. In seconds, the entire march descended on Ashima and prolonged the beating, taking turns.

When Ashima stopped moving, they spat on her and smashed the cafe's front windows. The men dropped their signs and ran, like cowards. As they disappeared around a bend, the cafe employees slowly emerged to check on the broken customer in their doorway.

✄

Seth went to the bar rather than home. Her favorite spot had a large outdoor patio, large enough for her to feel comfortable removing her mask. There was no joy behind her choice; she walked there to avoid Ashima's research. If a tiny portal opened in the looming Athens dusk, she'd have leapt through, sight unseen. Small glasses of whiskey neat began to pile up and the bar's sound personnel started testing mics and stage monitors for the evening's entertainment. Seth wanted no part of the mob. The maskless, coughing, inebriated assholes turned her stomach. She drank her final slug and pulled her mask back across her face to walk into the bar.

The bartender didn't acknowledge Seth when she dropped off the empty glasses, so she asked...

"Everything ok? You look..."

"No. It's fucking horrible..."

The bartender turned her phone:

UGA Astronomy Student attacked in Arizona during alleged Hate Crime

Seth dialed Ashima immediately. No answer. She dialed the Lowell Observatory. No answer. She dialed the Astronomy department...

"Hello, University of..."

"Have you heard from Ashima today?"

"No, they didn't tell you?"

"Tell me you've seen her. Tell me now!"

"I'm so sorry..."

Seth dropped her phone on the filthy barfloor.

><

Ashima's family in south Georgia kept a tight lock on her funeral. Seth was not invited, most of her friends and family from school were explicitly not invited. Ignorant savages murdered Ashima, and her family continued their terror by trying to erase her adult life.

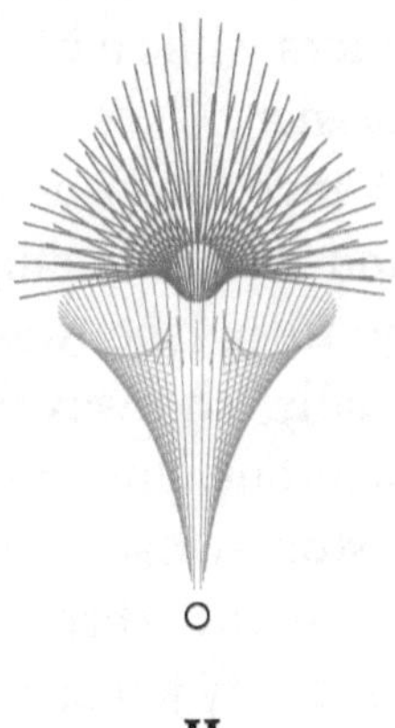

II

Dr. Basil's research was very detailed, but as he mentioned, it lacked coherence. The density of the notes and the breadth of the investigation plagued Ian's mind all day and long into sleep. He rose every hour, on the hour, until he finally gave up and prepared a press of coffee. As the blistering water soaked the ground beans, a strong wind outside crept into ancient fissures and played the sideboards of the old house like an instrument, creating a numb chorus, like a flurry of dead pages.

The bulk of the investigative evidence came from a small-town South Carolina journalist. An anonymous source sent this journalist photos of the infamous Judge Smalls Jr. at a lynching. One that took place at the massive Water Oak in Ian's backyard. Proud as a peacock in a pure white suit, hat, and tie, Judge Smalls' dearest legitimate son smiled for the camera while a young woman hung from the lowest branch.

The journalist made it clear that this should be a damning and career-ending photo, but it wasn't. At every turn, she was told it never happened. Eventually, she was warned that her curiosity was dangerous. But she persisted. After a shady traffic stop—what was she doing in Carnesville?—she spent three nights in the massive medium security jail on the edge of town.

According to her newspaper, she was never heard from again. No security footage was submitted of her getting into the car or leaving the property. It was never even mentioned. Ian closed down his laptop. Everyone seemed a little too calm. None of what he read felt like a coincidence.

⚔

It was a relief to have a little bit of money. The water department had been quite lenient and Ian did not want to push his luck.

The squat, brick municipal building housing the Carnesville Water Department had a narrow lobby area and several offices behind closed doors. A woman sat quietly reading a magazine at a long counter.

"Hello." Ian smiled.

The woman looked up slowly, "Yeah, what do you need..." Her eyes widened as they met Ian's. "Why are you here?"

"I'm here to pay my water bill." He was confused. "Can I do that here?"

"You're livin in th' Judge's house."

"So I hear." Ian replied.

"Ain't nobody supposed to live there. It's forbidden."

"Please, here is my card, just run the bill."

The woman rose from her stool, getting uncomfortably close to Ian. She was much taller than he expected, and her long, pale fingers were bent and gnarled by disease.

"Back off lady, you're being really fucking weird..."

The woman slammed her hands on the counter, "You aren't supposed to be there. No one is supposed to be there." She flung her head back and shrieked with many voices, "Blasphemer, you will bring about the cleansing fire..."

A door behind the counter opened and a tall elderly man emerged, wrapped his gangly arms around the woman's shoulders and drug her out of the room. She begged for mercy behind the closed door and suddenly went silent.

A younger man walked through the door next, closing it behind him. This man was neither tall nor short and had a salesman's demeanor.

"I apologize. How may I be of service?"

"I just want to pay the water bill. Is that woman alright?"

"Of course. I'll run your card. Just a moment." The young man turned and watched a small monitor after he swiped the card. "Ok, you are all set. 255 Athens Street is all paid up."

"Thank you. Hey," Ian turned back. "Are you sure she's okay?"

"Yes. She'll be just fine."

"Will I be fine?"

"What do you mean, Mr. Mhealladh?"

"She was very upset that someone was living in the Judge's old house."

The young man smirked at the mention of the Judge. "I assure you that she is out of sorts, but otherwise a typical old woman, nothing of a threat. Is there anything else I can help you with?"

"No, but thank you." Ian found that assertion hard to take on faith. Something was wrong with the people of Carnesville.

Professor Thoiaker wrapped his knuckles against the office door. "Seth. May I come in?"

Seth rose from her chair, startled by the intrusion. "Yes. Hello, Søren."

They shook hands cordially. "I cannot fathom what you are feeling right now, but if you need anything..."

"Thank you. I'm taking some time off."

"I'm being sincere. Do not hesitate to reach out."

Seth nodded. "I finished reviewing those bizarre papers for you. I'll drop my notes in the share drive."

"Oh, those were Dr. Basil's papers. He was specific about wanting you to review them. He didn't mention it?"

"No. That's strange, isn't it?"

"Dr. Basil has been a little strange lately. He's not taking this recent news about Ashima's attack very well."

"Murder."

"Yes, my apologies, murder. That's why I came to speak to you. Dr. Basil feels strongly that a local religious group is linked to the suspects in Arizona. Do you know where he's gotten this notion?"

"No, that's the first I've heard it mentioned."

"He's already hired someone to look into this group. Apparently, the man in the video footage had a tattoo that Dr. Basil recognized."

"Wait, you're saying that maniac lives in Georgia?"

"We don't know that for certain. This particular group seems to have gone quiet some time ago. Besides, these obscure sects of Christianity don't historically behave..."

Seth was not amused. "When did Dr. Basil intend to speak to me?"

"I can't say. I came to you of my own volition."

"Then I'll speak to Dr. Basil in person."

The doctor sat alone in his office reviewing a large book. Seth watched him for a moment. His movements were rhythmic, he was praying. Both of his hands trembled as if bearing a heavy weight, and his eyes were pressed shut.

"Please come in, Seth."

Seth was startled. "Pardon the interruption, Doctor."

"No pardon necessary. I very much wanted to speak to you. How are you feeling?"

"Okay. Not great. Some time off will help."

"Of course. It can't hurt. It's all so insane, I can't believe Ashima is gone. I can't believe her life was cut so short."

"It was very sudden I had just spoken to her..."

"About her research?"

"Yes, partly. She was most concerned about a date she had."

"Oh. Was she meeting with someone about her findings?"

"No, it seemed casual. Flirtatious."

"But she must have mentioned something."

"Not that I recall." *And if I did, I certainly wouldn't tell you.* "Was she working on something for you, Dr. Basil?"

"No, nothing like that. I am merely trying to piece together why all of this happened. I must know what she found, it is of the utmost importance. If you are keeping anything from me, you should reconsider."

When Seth explained she knew less than he did, Dr. Basil changed the subject. He showed her images and documents regarding a cult in rural Georgia that pledged allegiance to "The Keeper of Time." He was convinced that the cult had evolved into an extremist group.

As far as Seth was concerned, Dr. Basil's hunch was pretty weak. One of the bastards that took Ashima's life had an ancient icon tattooed across his neck, a lion-headed serpent with "Keeper of Time—Watcher of All That Is," scrawled as a coarse border around the image.

"This cult believes that the Keeper of Time is the creator of the material world. The weakness, arrogance, and greed of our species are due to this beast's dark nature."

"Why worship a god like that?"

"Power."

"So Ashima is just collateral damage in their struggle."

"I think her murder was symbolic. We have to stop these people, Seth. This isn't a war of words anymore."

Seth felt a bitter cold descend on the room, it was no longer safe. "If Ashima's research is made available to me, I will not hesitate to share it with you."

Dr. Micah Basil smiled, "Please see that you do, Seth. Run along now, I know you have much to attend to."

✄

Seth shared a weathered Victorian house with Ashima far from the campus. They didn't really share the place because Ashima was constantly on the other side of the country. As Seth wandered their large, empty home, she heard a voice. Faint at first, but as she strained to listen, it became more bold.

"Who are you?"

It did not answer when called.

Seth shouted, "Answer me!"

The house went black, every lamp extinguished and the slim crescent moon's albedo was pale and weak. She groped around until she found her phone and lit the way to the breaker box beneath the stairs. Each movement was amplified by the darkness, and the wide hall and high ceilings conjured phantom noises throughout the house.

Seth was not alone. She wanted to call out again, but decided not to succumb to madness. She noticed the air become cooler, more still. The hall before her remained a great black void too dense for her phone's flashlight to penetrate.

How long have I been walking? The breaker should have been a few steps away. Seth turned slowly, walking in several directions hoping to find the walls.

Her beam of light finally trained on a surface. The walls were the same, pale green trimmed in dark grey, cracked where they had always been. Seth had walked through empty space for an eternity before finding the hall's boundary, and now she saw only pale green walls stretching endlessly into the distance wherever she pointed her light.

As suddenly as the house had gone dark, it was bathed with penetrating light. The sun rose in every tall antique window, turning night instantly into day. Seth sprinted for the front door, flung it open, and stared skyward in horror. The night was pricked by ancient starlight, the texture of inky and infinite death. The tall pines concealing her house from the street were dimly lit by the waning moon.

When Seth walked back into the house, a bright, summer day blasted the windows with light. She had no friend to call, no family to offer her consolation. Now that Ashima was gone, she was alone with her madness.

As days and nights passed, Seth refused to leave the house for fear her hallucinations might persist in the outside world. The tiny voice in her head begged her to return to the data Ashima had compiled. The voice was certain some clue lay within those complex equations, some rendering of reality that would make it all worthwhile; would make it all make sense.

There's a hole in Eridanus. If it's a smaller void, it's like nothing we've seen before. There's something about this void that gives me the creeps. Which is dumb, I know. There's no evidence of matter within, and there are no markers of a black hole. It's just empty, Seth. Emptier than anything we've seen. We have to tighten up this data before we publish it. I want to be cautious. This is it, my friend. This may be the end.

On first review, her work made a compelling case for a region devoid of matter within the Eradinus super massive void. If the calculations were correct, it would be the first time humanity had witnessed a completely empty void. It would make more sense that this region's proximity to Eridanus, and its uniquely low galaxy density only made it appear to be devoid of matter. Contrary to popular belief, space tends to be not-empty as soon as you have the power to zoom in.

The work was immaculate and creative. Ashima had overcome many difficult questions that would arise from her conclusions. Seth was surprised by a hasty conclusion in one of the calculations. The tiny voice grew coercive. *Ashima did not make a mistake. She was hiding something.* Seth adjusted the equations and revised Ashima's computer models. The void was empty, more so than Ashima had originally calculated, but there was something else. Although no light escaped from or passed through this void, subtle fluctuations in its border regions looked like... movement. Variations in the positions of neighboring galaxies mimicked an object pushing out but being kept within. It didn't make any sense.

Seth could not concentrate, and the math began to fall apart. Tomorrow, she promised, I'll be in a better place.

Skippy's Lawn Service was the only crew within one hundred miles that did house calls. Paying money to cut grass that would inevitably grow back broke Ian's heart, but it mattered to the landlord. The lawn had grown up to near waist height; it was not going to be cheap.

Skippy himself came out to the property to give an assessment. He wasn't wearing a mask, but he didn't make a big deal about Ian's mask. They walked the property and Ian pointed out areas with large tree stumps that would be murder on a mower.

"Just up here, to the tree line. The owners asked that we keep the cleared area mowed, so feel free to skirt around the trees but stop when they get thick."

"Sure, no problem." Skippy had been quiet, letting Ian lead the conversation. "What brought you to Carnesville? If you don't mind my asking."

"Well, Athens felt a bit too crowded and I've always wanted to have a lot of space to kind of stretch out."

"You made a good choice. This is a very quiet community, not much in the way of traffic or excitement. Are you from Georgia?"

"No, Nevada, originally. My dad was in the military, so I've moved around quite a bit."

"Oh. Well, thank him for his service."

"I will." Definitely not.

"This house has a lot of history." Skippy started walking back to his truck. "Was built for the Judge a long way back."

"People point that out often. It's a beautiful house. Kind of a shame that they tore out the insides."

Skippy seemed suddenly concerned with the house. "What do you mean?"

"Well, they pulled all the walls down and replaced them with drywall. The fireplaces are laid out in piles just beyond the treeline. The charm was yanked out in favor of apartment-grade interiors. They even laid carpet."

Skippy grimaced. "Well, that happens sometimes. Hey, if you're the church going type, we have what you'd call a non-denominational flock right here in town..."

Skippy needed to work on his pitch delivery. "That's kind of you, but no thanks. Tell me more about the Judge."

"Sure thing. Judge Smalls ran things around here for a while. Parts of his family still run things. He stuck this house right down from city hall, and painted it canary yellow so that anyone passing through town saw his house first and City Hall second."

"I'm kind of surprised the judge would allow another house this close to his." Ian pointed to his neighbor. "Nice big house too."

"Christian and Bernette have lived there for as long as I can remember, but that used to be the widow Lungren's place, built a couple of decades after the judge built this house. The widow had seven children, rumor around town was that the three youngest belonged to the Judge. When the rumors got to be too much, all of a sudden the widow came into some money and built a house, right next to the Judge."

Ian laughed. "Convenient."

"Oh yes. The Judge had his trouble with women."

"Married a lot?"

"Four times. And three of 'em up and left in the middle of the night. Never to return."

"That seems a bit..."

"Yep. Rumor has it he buried 'em in this yard so no one'd ever know." Skippy smiled, it wasn't often a stranger wanted to hear the mythos of Carnesville. "Well, we're burnin' daylight, so I'll quit talkin' your ear off. The first round will be $425—there's a lot to clear away. After that, I'll come every other week; for $75 I'll keep it tidy for you."

"Ouch. When are you thinkin'?"

"I brought some help with me, we can get started now."

Ian shook his hand. "Perfect."

"We should be done in a few hours, I'll knock and let you know."

The yard became a flurry of green, with a din of noise rising from deafening gas engines. Skippy rode in large circles around the overgrown back acre—leaning dramatically as his riding mower cleared crop circles behind the imperious white house. His partner tended to the edges and along the driveway.

Skippy seemed very concerned with what the new owners had done to the house. Christian also seemed very protective of the Judge's property. According to the neighbor, the only part of the house that hadn't been touched was the basement crawlspace.

Ian removed a heavy boulder that kept the door leading beneath the house secure. The space was divided into rooms, with each step Ian kicked up red dust and loose rocks.

The first room was lit by a pair of windows beneath the house floors, and had a single folding chair sitting at its center. It looked out of place, like an interrogation. The breaker box was on the last wall Ian scanned. Ian got closer to read the labels and something cold touched his bare neck.

He dropped to the dirt floor and scanned the bowels of the house. Above his head hung a limp, discarded skin from a long Black Snake. The voided scales were wrapped around several pipes running beneath the floorboards. Even though there was no longer a snake in that skin, it meant that Ian was not alone.

He walked deeper into the crawlspace, finding darkened room after room until he stumbled on a lit room. A crumbling stone well that someone had recently packed with mud and debris dominated the center of the space. Ian searched for a light switch but could not find one.

The light turned off and it was impossible to see.

"Okay...thanks?"

The light turned back on. Then off. Then on, again and again, filling the dank crawlspace with dirty strobing light. Ian was suddenly gripped by terror, his heart raced and his head throbbed, he was not alone. Ian sprinted from the room and crouched next to the crawlspace windows to catch his breath.

Skippy and his partner had already cleared the back half of the yard when a shriek of grinding metal scattered buzzards from the trees. The blades from Skippy's riding mower shattered, sending deadly shrapnel across the freshly hewn yard. A thick spray of crimson exploded onto the sun-drenched driveway as jagged iron eviscerated Skippy's partner and blasted through the walls of the house.

Skippy leapt from the mower, trying to dial 911 as he bound toward his thrashing employee. He did his best to hold the man's insides together and screamed the house address into his cell phone.

Ian watched silently through the crawlspace windows while Skippy begged his friend to hold on.

"Yes, hurry, please...I don't know, I heard a loud sound and his chest just burst open, I don't know...No, I don't think he was shot...He was trimming the lawn." Skippy's mind returned to him, "Something from the lawn mower hit him. I think that's what happened."

Skippy looked into his employee's empty eyes and sobbed. "Oh no. He's dead. He's fucking dead."

Franklin County Sheriff's deputies conducted their investigation rapidly. The riding lawn mower struck a piece of granite hidden by the tall grass, causing it to hurl metal across the yard. The Sheriff's deputies left a card for a cleaning crew. The evidence of butchery tinting the driveway with red was Ian's responsibility now.

There was no spare money for professional services, so the wide splashing mark blackened and refused to retreat. It became easier to ignore the bloodstains as the days passed, but it was ever present, marring the glorious midday sunlight.

When Seth descended the staircase, Ashima's body lay prone on the dining table. Seth could not move. She dared not speak, lest the apparition become real. Ashima shuddered and raised her body up with her arms, leaving her legs limp. *Seth. I have come back.*

This was not Ashima. Seth begged her legs to run, to flee this abomination.

But it is Ashima. Your Ashima, Seth. Do not forsake me.

Seth wept.

The imposter folded down from the dining table, swinging with unnatural, insect gestures. Ashima's flesh and bones were there, guided and manipulated by an unseen force.

"You're scaring me."

Don't be so fragile, Ashima hissed. *We cannot conform to niceties. We come to you with great effort and danger to my eternal person.*

"What are you?"

We are your friend and your most secret desire. We are why you know things no one else can. Don't you recognize me? Ashima's face softened—from condescending to conniving.

"I do not believe you. I will never believe you. Ashima is gone."

My options for communicating with you are limited. We are your Ashima, but this flesh is no more. Your memories are my only palette. If you look at me and feel fear, you are to blame.

The creature settled into a Lotus position at Seth's feet. It was getting better at mimicking Ashima.

Seth continued to recall Ashima in moments of bliss and beauty to refine the entity's incarnation of her murdered friend. "That's better."

Thank you. We are better together.

"I want no part of this, Ashima. I cannot be a party to this madness."

It's too late, Seth. Our destiny is to learn of our destruction, to understand what is to come.

"Nothing is inexorable."

We have found that to be false. When you see reality from the heights of the ancients, you understand that our tiny bubble of chance and chaos fits neatly into an external frame of unbending progress.

The walls and ceiling of the house started to shatter and break apart with great wrenching and smashing. Seth dropped to the ground and covered her head. Terrible heat washed over her body and hung around her like a scalding bath. Seth slowly pulled her hands away from her eyes. Blinding light and colors she could not define consumed everything around her. As her vision adjusted, she could make out undulating shapes, like distant ripples in newborn gas clouds. She peered into a universe in eternal flux, an ever-flowing state resisting the descent into matter.

What we consider real is an illusion. Our material reality is not the rule, it is an aberration. These are not new sentiments. But now we see that this aberration is a tumor that has been quarantined. Our experience, this universe we have studied so closely, cannot be allowed to infect reality. We discovered something we should not have, Seth. The reason for this quarantine, and the impetus for our failed universe, is trapped in Eradinus.

"The movement."

Yes.

"But that's just an assumption."

The correct assumption. The vile thing being contained in that void is our reason for existing, and will soon be the reason we all perish.

"How do we stop it?"

You are very certain of your own power. Be warned, it is an illusion. We unveiled something beyond our understanding, a trapped god. This beast is emerging, and once it is free, all that we know will perish. Your discovery means that the future has already been written.

"Ashima did not discover a trapped god. She discovered a void. An unprecedented cosmic structure, but not...that."

This beast needed you to discover its prison cell. It learns as we learn. Its understanding of our reality is fed by our observation. This ancient evil could not escape without knowing the nature of its captivity, and it was blind without our curiosity.

"What does it want?"

Freedom. And then revenge. The great anchor placed around its neck warped Reality, creating a deep well from which nothing can escape. For an eternity, the child god stared out from within this prison.

"Observation changes the experiment."

Observation fixes reality. This creature's unmoving gaze—observing the quantum dance—forced energy to choose states and eventually collapse into particles— material reality. As the fetal strands of our webbed universe formed, the beast never averted its gaze. Every atom in our reality is in place because of its unblinking vigilance and rage. Its constant scrutiny caused great and powerful collisions of matter, shattering into innumerable galaxies and stars. This beast is not our creator, that is a lie, but if it looks away or becomes distracted, all matter will become formless.

"Formless, like this?" Seth gestured to the bright chaos all around her.

Yes. For a time. Some will be eviscerated in a blink of destruction—for that, they can be thankful. Those left to witness the beast's ascent gain nothing but the choking madness of being drowned in raw reality. As one begins to understand that there is no consciousness outside of the beast's gaze, madness sets in—an ancient, existential madness—that prepares the human mind to view the rudderless and chaotic reality beyond our own.

Ian stayed inside, but when the milk and cheese ran out he was forced to leave the house. It was sunny and hopeful outside, it finally felt right to leave. The granite marker that murdered Skippy's partner was sunlit through the trees. It looked like it had writing on it. No one had mentioned writing. Ian pulled at a tangle of branches until he reached the marker. Its grey, speckled surface was marred by a deep white scar from the mower blade. It read simply *Here rests a liar.*

The nearest proper grocery experience was thirty miles away so the people of Carnesville relied on DollarVine, a popular discount store that was smart enough to include a refrigerated section. There were no fruits or vegetables in sight and prices were inflated for the full convenience store experience, but the people of Carnesville had no other choice.

Ian pulled his mask on and entered the grim fluorescent retail nightmare. He secured the necessities and a few little treats.

The lady at the DollarVine register was always there, night and day.

"Hey."

"How's your day?" Ian asked.

"Almost over."

Ian smiled, but she couldn't tell. He tried to ignore her t-shirt: *Anti-vax is the new black.*

"That's $54.26. Sorry."

"Wow. You don't need to apologize, but the people who set these prices should..."

"I know. It ain't right."

Ian's transaction was approved. "Well, you have a good one."

"You know you don't have to wear those things on your face, right? It was all a big hoax. No one 'round here fell for it." She smiled strangely and a chill fell over the store.

Ian felt very uncomfortable. "Better safe than sorry. There's too much risk."

"Yeah, that's all fine, but it was a lie. Demons in the government wanted all of us to lose touch, mask ourselves so we weren't human no more. So we'd be easier to control. After all, if they can get you to deny your own god-given-humanity by wearing a mask, they can get your soul."

Ian saluted politely and walked out the door. The townspeople were escalating; perhaps it was best to stay in after all. As if the clouds were eavesdropping on his thoughts, a hard rain fell from the sky. Ian walked carefully to his car—surely the rain was a clear sign to stay in.

※

Ian read his email to Søren a third time, it sounded outrageous; far-fetched was too kind. The journalist's notes left plenty of hints; the connection was difficult to uncover, but not impossible. It felt a little too easy, like Dr. Basil had handed him a foregone conclusion pretending to be a puzzle. Ian decided that tipping his hand to Søren first was less risky, and keeping his insights to himself was far too risky. His friend's reaction to the email would tell him everything he needed to know.

> *Søren,*
> *The cult didn't go underground, it became political. Once they got a taste of power, they had a change of heart about bringing the apocalypse. Under a corporate moniker "The Six Sisters", they maintain an economic stranglehold on the entire county. This entity generates profit by renting prison labor to corporations, and has a vested interest in making sure that the apocalypse never comes. From what I can tell, they've been purposely running outsiders off since the 1960s to protect their secret. They're stalling.*

Ian pressed send.

The rain continued steadily until night fell. Lightning began to flash and was immediately accompanied by a series of intense booms. Ian turned the light off in his office and watched streaks of light paint massive black storm clouds with quicksilver. The terrible storm would not relent, it seemed to heave and puff its chest for onslaught.

As Ian walked down the stairs, white light from the backyard blinded him and a deafening crack rattled the windows. Fire from the sky split an immense oak down the center of its trunk, sending its thick branches crashing to the ground. The sudden weight caved in part of the yard and an explosion in the crawlspace shook the house. Small glowing fires in the fallen limbs simmered but were kept at bay by the heavy rain.

The crawlspace beneath the house was dark and the muddy floor was uneven. The door leading to the well was shattered and lay in pieces. Debris exploded to the surface of the well when the yard collapsed, and the room was filled knee-deep with sludge.

Ian could hear wind passing through the bottom of the well. The sound had to lead somewhere, he now knew his purpose.

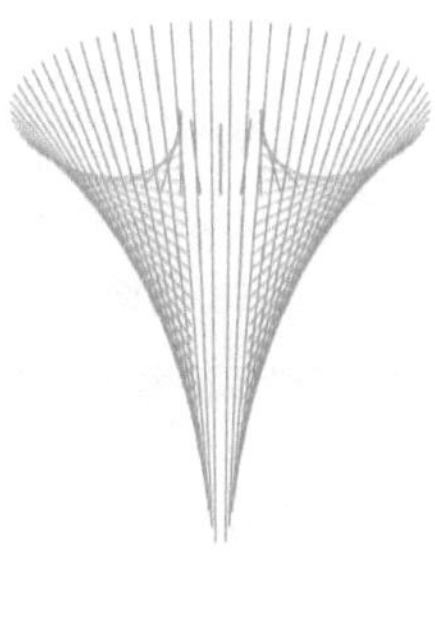

III

Søren texted Ian.

—Hey, can I give you a call?

Ian began to cry. Exhaustion. Shame. He didn't know if he could speak to another person.

Søren texted, —I think it's easier to speak than to write it out in messages.

—Okay, Ian responded.

"Ian. Thank you for taking my call. The information you sent me this week led to a lot of strange revelations. Are you there?"

Ian murmured. "Yes. I'm here."

"Good. You were correct, the cult didn't go underground, it put on a corporate disguise. Their companies thrive on no-bid government contracts and peddling extremist merchandise. Not to sound all tinfoil hat, but this supposedly non-existent group of corporations has underwritten everything from political families, to call centers."

"That tracks, but so what?"

"I think you are in danger. Dr. Basil is clearly involved. The documents from that journalist tie his name to the Six Sisters. I don't think we can trust him."

"How did I miss that?"

"You didn't, Dr. Basil hid it well. I've heard him tell stories about his vacation home on Lake Hartwell for years. That's the only reason I recognized the address in the property reports."

"Why did he choose me?" Ian sounded terrified.

"I chose you."

"Yes, I think that was part of the plan all along. Did he mention anything else?"

"Just that he thought someone outside of the university would be more objective. Anyone taking a paycheck from the school would have a conflict of interest." Søren paused. "He knew this entire time."

"He knew I would be close to the source. Close to whatever he thinks I'll find here. Dr. Basil doesn't care about the cult, he wants to bring their apocalypse."

"You should leave immediately. Come here and we can put you up until this gets sorted out."

"I can't. I'm very close."

"Don't be insane, we need to report Dr. Basil to the authorities. You have to get as far away as you can, everything leads back to that house."

"That's why I can't leave."

"...Ian?"

The university had been very kind to Seth. In part because of Ashima's tragic death, but primarily because the virus made it bad PR to force tenured staff into a high risk environment. The student body came from all cardinal points and mingled with passion for four to eight years; social distancing was not on the agenda.

She was pleasantly surprised when her key card still unlocked the department doors. Seth's colleague, Dr. Antigone, sat quietly in the staff lounge eating ramen noodles and scanning a magazine.

Seth pointed to the magazine. "Anything interesting?"

Dr. Antigone smiled. "Yes, actually. The Euyin Deep Space Telescope had to change course three years ago, the article doesn't mention why. Strange. Anyway, as a result, it's going to capture redshift imagery from the Eradinus supervoid."

It can't be a coincidence. Seth felt her heart begin to race. "When?"

"Um," Dr. Antigone scanned the article and checked her watch. "Oh, they'll begin collecting data today, actually."

"Evelynn. I called you because I need your help. This is the most important thing I've ever asked for, and I can't take no for an answer. I'm continuing Ashima's work, and I need you to gut check my calculations. I can't trust myself. I can't trust my..."

"Objectivity. Seth, you're scaring me."

"I'm fine, Evelynn. Please. Help me. Help Ashima. This research is what made her stay in that godless desert."

Dr. Antigone stood, preparing to leave. "Seth. I can see that you are in pain, but I would not have driven down here if I knew you intended to..."

"Sit down." Seth shoved the doctor back into her chair. "I'm experiencing vivid hallucinations and I need to know if you see what I see. It's even more important that this data be verified before we point the Euyin telescope at Eradinus."

"Seth, I don't believe you intend to hurt me. I'm going to leave now and I swear to you, I won't mention this to anyone."

Seth backhanded Dr. Antigone, splitting her lip. "I need your help." Seth pulled her jacket back to reveal a pistol Ashima had kept in the house *because we live in Georgia.*

Dr. Antigone wiped blood from her mouth. "This is madness, Seth. Think of your career."

"My career died when that maniac murdered Ashima. Either I've gone mad..."

"Or?"

"Or everything we know and love is about to end violently. There is something inside of that void. Something that is trying to escape. I can hear it in my thoughts."

"I'll run the models for you, but I won't do it at gunpoint."

"I'll keep the gun holstered." Seth snapped a pair of handcuffs around Dr. Antigone's wrist and the steel arm of her chair. "I brought your laptop from the lab. Please, get to work. I don't know what will happen when the Euyin makes its pass, but it's important. I can feel it."

Seth would not sleep, and she refused to let Dr. Antigone do more than nap. At the end of the third day, the doctor begged for a short reprieve. *She's going to try to escape. You should not trust her. This is a mistake.*

Seth considered it for a long time before unholstering her gun and unlocking Dr. Antigone. "Don't make me regret this."

The exhausted doctor agreed and Seth walked her out into the frigid night air. A deep layer of summer snow had fallen while they remained in the windowless department.

Dr. Antigone trudged into it, smiling for the first time in days. "This is a bizarre surprise."

Seth watched her carefully. "Doesn't make any sense. It wasn't even cold today."

"Do you mind if I smoke, Seth?"

"That shit is bad for you."

"So is having a pistol pointed at your back."

"Ok. Slowly."

The doctor pulled a cigarette from her breast pocket and lit it. "Sure you don't want one?"

"Positive."

After several long inhalations, the doctor turned her head. "The good news is that you aren't mad. The anomaly Ashima discovered is unprecedented. It's like nothing I've ever seen, like anyone has ever seen." The doctor inhaled deeply and watched the dense cloud of smoke hang in the freezing air. "The bad news is, what scares you most pans out in the data. There is an erratic pulse, a push and pull that seems to validate your hypothesis. A very powerful force is trying to escape this region and is being drawn back by a much stronger force. Phenomena on this scale should take millions of years to play out, which means we're missing something. These immense forces do not appear to have a warping effect on the rest of the Eradinus supervoid, as if it is cut off, protected from everything around it."

"Or we're being protected from whatever is inside."

"It's more likely that Ashima discovered an ancient singularity, closer to the beginning of the universe than anything viewed thus far."

"Something put it there. Something powerful trapped whatever this thing is, to punish it, and now it wants to escape."

"Where are you getting all of this nonsense? Our universe doesn't *trap* distant objects to punish them. I feel strongly that if we observe Eradinus for a longer period of time, we'll discover an ancestor of the supermassive black holes we observe today. It's far too early to make clear determinations. I'm sure with some more time and a research team we could..."

"It's too late for that. Listen to me. Something is trying to leave that void. I don't know what that means, or how I know it. But I'm scared. Ashima told me that this is the end."

"The universe will not end crushed by an ancient monster, it will end as all things do—in its time." Dr. Antigone looked at her watch again. Over her shoulder, she whispered, "The Euyin just completed its pass. Dozens of teams are analyzing the data as we speak."

Seth began to sob. Her weeping body shook and heaved as tears overwhelmed. "It was all for nothing, Evelynn. Everything, every human life, every sentient thought, meant nothing. It is finished."

Dr. Antigone drove her elbow into Seth's face, causing her to drop the pistol in the snow. When the pain subsided and Seth's vision returned, Dr. Antigone had the pistol trained on her head.

"I'm going to call the police. You need help, Seth. I'm sorry, but I can't let you...let you..."

"You can't shoot me is what you mean." Seth's eyes were wild with rage as she began advancing toward Dr. Antigone.

The doctor pulled the trigger. Both were surprised when it did not fire. Seth tackled Dr. Antigone to the ground and tried to turn her wrist. Instead of freeing the firearm, she caused it to discharge. Seth gushed thick, dark blood from a massive wound near her stomach.

Dr. Antigone held the gun at her side, backing away slowly. Seth crawled across the fresh white snow, painting it crimson. She collapsed before she could reach Dr. Antigone.

All is lost if I am found. Ian started digging in the well and could not stop. He summoned an inhuman stamina and dug night and day. When he reached the base of the shallow well, he could still see trickles of daylight coming through the cellar windows. This light illuminated the bottom of the well, but naught else. A lantern was all Ian had when darkness fell. He continued digging away from the well, beneath the yard, and the lantern became his only solace. *All is lost unless I am found.*

✕

"Hello, down there! Ian?" The next door neighbor called from the top of the well. "It's Christian, from next door. You never dropped by the church. We kinda hoped...well, here's the thing, your backdoor was unlocked, I wanted to make sure everything is okay."

That was a lie. The house had been locked up tight for days.

"All the noise down here made me suspicious."

Ian slowly extinguished his lantern and lay in wait.

"Are you down here?" Christian called out again into the darkness. "Answer me..." he raised his voice but quickly recovered, "Truth be told, you really shouldn't be messin' around down here. It's dangerous. I just want to make sure you are safe."

When Christian was met by silence, he struggled to lower himself down into the shallow well. He peered down the tunnel Ian carved into the red Georgia clay and snapped his fingers to judge its depth. "If you're hurt, just call out, I can help." Christian walked deeper into the tunnel, feeling the walls with both hands and stepping carefully. "I don't want you to jump to any conclusions here, Ian. This is a good, moral community. All we want is to live in peace."

The neighbor was backlit by weak clementine rivulets of setting summer sunlight. Ian watched as his neighbor approached blindly, staring into a tunneling void of bleak darkness.

"Our lord personally works through every one of us, neighbor. He feels everything we feel and listens to our most secret thoughts." Christian shouted, "You do not know what you are fucking with, Ian! You have no power here. My lord will torture your flesh for eternity. Agony forever awaits all blasphemers."

When Christian was close enough to smell, Ian attacked, creasing his neighbor's forehead with his heavy iron spade. Christian moaned and tried to crawl away.

Ian relit his lantern. "Why did you come here, neighbor? You've complicated things..."

Perhaps this is a gift. A sacrifice.

Ian stared down at his bleeding neighbor.

He intended to harm you. His wife will wonder where he is, but you can't let him live. Not now.

Ian pressed his heavy boot against Christian's chest to steady him on his back. "I am sparing you this madness. What is to come, cannot be undone."

Ian brought the spade down hard on his neighbor's throat and metal struck the packed soil beneath. Blood blanketed the walls and the lantern, casting the tunnel in a menacing red.

You can trust revelations born of violence. Your people have always known this.

Ian pushed Christian's head aside and buried his spade into the dark soil. He began slowly, carefully marking out the edge of another tunnel —down, deeper into...what? *Leading to the truth, Ian. Leading to the answers. Leading to whatever has this place under its spell. We've come too far to stop.*

"We?"

Yes, we.

Ian did not speak, he responded by digging. And digging.

⋈

A gash in the clay sighed as air rushed into the tunnel. Ian hacked at the rock and mud, widening the gap, but was overcome by a paralyzing stench. After emptying his stomach onto the tunnel floor, Ian continued to pull and hack at the remaining rock and mud until he was able to step through the hole. He entered a large chamber whose low ceilings were raw earth, invaded by errant root systems with no hint of sunlight.

The overwhelming smell brought waves of nausea and Ian struggled to walk deeper into the chamber. The crude walls and ceiling were petulant, a rushed, careless sanctuary whose filthy cement floors were scrawled with bizarre symbols in thick red paint. He lifted his flashlight and discovered the room's grim purpose.

A massive pit filled with human remains consumed the center of the chamber. The man-made hole was cramped with arms, legs, and staring eyes—corpses in various stages of liquefaction and decay. The impenetrable gore and horror of this sloppy mass grave served no purpose but its master's pleasure—no evidence of respect, or reverence, or worship, just a death chamber of decomposing trophies.

Ian cried out and drove his spade into a wall. As he hacked away at the rock and mud, he revealed another tunnel. Digging deeper and deeper beneath the forest, he emerged in another room. This chamber, like the last, was burdened with a sickening pit tainted by endless rotting flesh discarded in macabre positions.

Each violent scene led to another tunnel, which revealed another more revolting massacre. The web of extermination pits beneath the city of Carnesville was endless. It was the place in our universe where the love of power, and the seduction of perversity were strongest. A fertile seedbed to foment a monster's resurrection story.

Ian would never escape. Where he fled, this curse would follow, and wherever he hid, his thoughts would be plagued.

⚔

Wrath has been unleashed—be it ever so silent. Beware, lest it seduce us into submission. There has been no terrible rending of reality, for that we remain grateful. Though we can all feel the beast among us, we know that its deceit extended to its claims of omnipotence.

Our god is An Awesome god

A god was one day discovered lying prone, nearly encased in the Earth. Its frightened face formed undulating prairies and low, winding hills. The terrified god was still as death, save its ability to speak. Having fallen from imperfect control of the known universe, the god was now a hapless, squawking prisoner of soil and human soles.

Competition was vicious in the forgotten, before times, when gods were myriad. It was this buried god, this weak-chinned ladder-climber that threw its lot in with humans. By invasion and manipulation, this god connived and bargained, raising cruel and destructive men to power. Vile edicts began to dominate the human mind, inspiring acts of self-mutilation and war, until the god set forth its most primal demand:

There shall be none above me.
By the spilling of blood,
Where there were many,
Now there is One.

Though the god could never directly challenge its peers, the depravity of humans under the god's influence conjured enough suffering to ensure its immortality. Feeding on our friction and sowing chaos kept its gluttonous belly full. Without darkness, true believers insisted, there can be no dawn. And so the god was excused for cruelty so that we may see the light.

⚔

This god, toppled from the throne we created, murmured through clenched teeth...

"Do not harm me."

"But we have so many reasons to harm you. To tear you to pieces. To drown you. Murder, and torture you."

"I am the source and the instigation all humanity seeks to understand. By cruel incantation of the Elders, I was made mute. I tried to reach out to you.

"I am your lord because I took control. I placed my hands around reality and protected you from chaos. It was not love that bore me subjects, it was my will. You were my prize. Do not harm me, I *command* you."

"You cannot punish us. You wield no power."

"I am your creator."

"You are our plague."

⚔

The sycophants attempted to militarily defend their god but they were no bulwark against the whole of humanity. Eventually, the god was squared in by several miles of velvet rope. Endless lines form each day for humans to sidle by and spit on the god, kick its granite teeth, and avenge the deaths of their loved ones.

Each day the god lies still, occasionally crying out, but resigned to its fate: prisoner to our punishment.

When, not if

Stars in the sky began to fade and disappear. Many more than we imagined in such a short increment of time. Weak, pale light receded until we were alone with our dying local star. It was assumed that "our" canopy of starlight, as known since ancient times, represented the final truth of the universe. We wept and tore our clothing when we lost the vibrant night sky, prostrated at the feet of an arbitrary view into the history of the universe.

As above, so below.

Acknowledgements

Unflinching praise and gratitude for Nate and Shaunn. The caring home you provide for my (deeply) blasphemous thoughts is greatly appreciated. If Westboro Baptist shows up at your homes, I'd like to formally apologize. Mad props to The Wife, who suffers through the earliest drafts of everything, and my incessant rambling about space, and time, and spacetime, and black holes (a lot of that, actually). Sincere thanks to Seb Doubinsky, Scott Gilbertson, Lindz McLeod, John Madera, Pam Jones, Jordan A. Rothacker, and Brandon Getz for reading this thing and sharing their impressions. Sympathy and solidarity with every person that resists the darkness this book seeks to illuminate.

About the Author

Enemy of every State.

About the Publishing Team

Nate Ragolia is a lifelong lover of science fiction and its power to imagine worlds more hopeful and inclusive than the real one. His first book, *There You Feel Free*, was published by 1888's Black Hill Press in 2015. Spaceboy Books reissued it in 2021. He's also the author of *The Retroactivist* (2017). His most recent book, *One Person Can't Make a Difference* (2022), was featured on Tor.com's Can't Miss Indie Press Speculative Fiction list, and was translated into Italian for Ringworld Sci-Fi in 2023. He founded and edited *BONED*, a literary magazine, and also created two webcomics. Nate is also a husband and a dog dad.

Shaunn Grulkowski has been compared to Warren Ellis and Phillip K. Dick and was once described as what a baby conceived by Kurt Vonnegut and Margaret Atwood would turn out to be. He's at least the fifth best Slavic-Latino-American sci-fi writer in the Baltimore metro area. He's the author *Retcontinuum*, and the editor of *A Stalled Ox* and *The Goldfish* for 1888/Black Hill Press.

www.ingramcontent.com/pod-product-compliance
Lightning Source LLC
Chambersburg PA
CBHW020802190726
48285CB00006B/2131